Rogg's BAR and GRILL

ROGER RIFFELMACHER

authorHOUSE®

AuthorHouse™
1663 Liberty Drive
Bloomington, IN 47403
www.authorhouse.com
Phone: 1 (800) 839-8640

Published by AuthorHouse 06/10/2016

ISBN: 978-1-5246-1329-7 (sc)
ISBN: 978-1-5246-1330-3 (hc)
ISBN: 978-1-5246-1328-0 (e)

CHAPTER 1

After being married for 43 good years, Roger's wife died unexpectedly; the house that they lived in was too big and lonely to live in by himself. It had too many memories of his wife, so he thought about selling it. Roger only had one son who was married with three children of his own. For the past couple of years Roger and his son Butch didn't see eye to eye on anything and grew apart. His son was too busy with his life, and raising his own family, so after some minor disagreements Roger and his son went their separate ways. Once his house was sold, there wasn't any reason to stay up there. In the winter it was too cold and in the summer there were too many bugs.

A week before he moved, Roger went around and said "good bye" to all his friends he had known. He had no idea where he was going yet, but it had to be warmer and fewer bugs than here. He loaded everything he could in his big old car and headed south. He was going to Florida. That's right, Florida, where the weather would be a lot warmer than here, and fewer bugs to put up with. "I'm free at last. Thank God Almighty, I'm free at last."

Two days after Roger left for Florida, a large black car pulled up in front of his old house. A man in his 50's and dressed mostly in black went up to his old house and inquired from the new owner where Roger had gone. The family inside said they didn't know. He hadn't left a forwarding address, except that it would be somewhere in Florida. So the stranger said "Thank you," and left.

Roger took his time driving south for the next two days. He did a little sightseeing along the way; in the morning he would sleep in, and at night he drank a few beers, now that he had all the time in the world now.

On the second day, he saw a black man in an Army Uniform hitch-hiking. So he pulled over and offered the young solder a ride. "Get in; I'm going south, all the way to Florida." Roger said; "How far are you going?"

"All the way to Georgia, mister, that's where I 'm from. I just spent eight long years in the Army, and now I'm going home, my name is Clyde." Roger smiled, then said, "Well

Clyde; I'm glad to meet you. Did you see much action while you were overseas?"

"Yah, I spent two tours in Iraq; when I made it through the second time without getting hurt. I figured I shouldn't push my luck any longer and I had enough. So I got out and now I'm going home."

"I always thought the Army gave you guys a ticket or something to get home on."

"They still do, but I lost mine playing cards with some of my buddies, you know how that goes."

"I sure do; I spent four years in the Air Force. Only I didn't see any action like you did; I just retired and now I'm going where I hope it'll be warm all the time. These old bones just can't take the cold anymore."

Roger and Clyde hit it off pretty well; they talked for the next three hours. It seemed like they had a lot in common. They talked about the time they spent in the military and the different sports they liked, and a lot about the women.

"I have to stop and get some gas pretty soon and we'll get a bite to eat at the next town we come to." Roger told Clyde.

About fifteen minute later stopped at a little town in the middle of nowhere. There was only one old gas station and a rundown restaurant. The gas station was on one side of the road and the restaurant was on the other side.

"Hey Clyde, why don't you go over and get us something to eat, and I'll be over as soon as I get some gas."

"Take your time; I'll get us something to chow down on." Clyde said as he walked across the street and into the greasy spoon where he ordered a couple hamburgers to go.

While Clyde was waiting for his food, he noticed two red-necks that were sitting in a booth; But he didn't' think anything about it, and sat down at the counter waiting for the food. The two red-necks got up and walked over to Clyde. One of the guys bumped into him on purpose, almost knocking him to the floor.

"What's wrong with you?" Clyde said to the two red-necks.

They both turned around and the biggest one, the one with the long hair said, "Hey Boy, are you a real soldier or are you just playing like one, so this old man will give you a free hamburger? You know what, I think you should take that uniform off Boy; there're too many white boys wearing the same uniform. I said "NOW" the red-neck yelled at Clyde."

Across the street Roger had just finished pumping his gas and went over to the greasy spoon to get his food. When he opened the door he saw that one of the red-necks was holding Clyde from behind and his friend with the long hair was about ready to hit him; Roger ran up behind the one that was getting ready to hit his friend, and grabbed him by his long hair, pulled him backward and down to the floor, in a flash Clyde turned around and punched the other guy in the face. In less than a second the two red necks took off running out the front door.

When the big one ran out the door, he yelled, "I'll be back."

Clyde looked at him and yelled back, "Run you chicken shits, run, and don't let the door hit your ass on the way out."

The old man that was behind the counter said "I'm sorry about what just happened, those two are a wild bunch" When the old man handed Roger and Clyde their food he told them, "They'd better take their food and leave because those red-nicks would be back with some of their friends. The food is on the house; now you guys had better get going."

"Thanks mister," Roger said as he took the food and left.

The day after Roger and Clyde left the greasy spoon, a large black car pulled into the gas station to fill up. After he got his gas the stranger walked across the street to get something to eat and maybe some information. When he asked the old man behind the counter if he saw a man that looked like Roger, the old man told the stranger he remembered seeing them alright, but he was a day too late.

After the stranger finished eating he walked back to his car; and the same two red-nicks stopped him and said. "After you get done with them two, we have some unfinished business with them, if you know what I mean;" The stranger just looked at the two red-necks and without saying a word, got into his car and left.

It didn't take long to drive though Tennessee. Then they came to Georgia, and Roger and Clyde would part company.

"You know buddy, if you're ever down in Florida, look me up and we'll have a beer or something,"

"I might just do that Roger; yep I'll take you up on that, but it'll be on me. By the way, how will I find you?"

"That's something I don't even know, I guess it depends on where I run out of gas or find a friendly bar."

"Well good luck and thanks for the lift." Clyde said.

The two bumped knuckles and Roger drove off. For some unknown reason he liked that guy. But little did Roger know that the guy in the big black car was getting closer, and closer.

CHAPTER 2

The closer Roger got to Florida the heavier the traffic became. When he finally got to Florida, he stopped at the first Welcome Center he came to. So he could pick up a map of the state and get a free glass of O.J. He made his way over to the Information Center and asked one of the ladies working there, "Is it always this busy?"

She just looked at him and nodded yes, "You're going in the wrong direction if you don't want to be around people."

"Wow, I never thought it would be like this. Where are they going?"

"The same place you're going sir, to get some of our Hot Florida sun."

"Man, I never thought it was going to be like this." He said thank you, and then walked over to a corner to study the map. The way he saw it he could drive south for four to five hours, than get off I-75.Than he would cruise around until he found someplace he liked, as long as the weather was warm, warm, warm.

After three days of sightseeing and driving up and down the state, he made his way to the Keys where he would stop for the night. It was a little place that was called, "Rogg's Bar and Grill." It looked like a small Ma and Pa type restaurant that catered to just the locals, the building was very small and needed a paint job. Hopefully something other than the pink and blue it was painted. The parking lot was made of gravel with large pot holes in it, just by looking at it you knew you wouldn't be overcharged. That's where he would eat tonight.

The day before a stranger in a big black car pulled into the parking lot and was going to get something to eat, but didn't stop because there were too many chickens running around in the parking lot, so he went to the next little island.

When Roger pulled into the parking lot a damn chicken ran out in front of his car and he squashed it. When he got out of the car, he looked at the dead bird then he saw a big arrow painted on the side wall of the building pointing to the back, saying, "Patio, this way." So he thought why not stay outside on the patio; this way he could enjoy eating in the warm Florida sun. There were only three tables on the patio and other customers sitting at two of them; Roger went over to the only empty one and sat down.

When the waitress came out, she was waving her arms in the air, and asked him, "Are you the one that just killed the chicken?" He didn't know what to say, so he sat there and studied the waitress. "Well, are you or aren't you?" she asked once again.

"Yah, I mean yes. It was an accident. I'll pay you for the bird if you want me to."

"No you won't," she said, than started to laugh. "Whoever kills a chicken here gets a free drink on the house. So now, are you the one that killed the chicken or not?"

"Yah the bird ran out in front of me and I couldn't stop."

"I don't care about how you did it, you'll get a free drink, so what'll it be?"

"I'll have a Bud Lite" Roger smiled at her; Alice disappeared back inside of "Rogg's Bar and Grill."

While he was waiting for his free beer and a hamburger to come out, a tall women about 5 ft. 10 in. more or less who was in her early sixties, walked over to his table and sat down on the opposite side of him. "So you're the Chicken Killer." she said half laughing; "I'm Judy, what might your name be, buster? I know just about everyone on this little island, and you're not from around here;" Judy knew that

Alice liked to kid strangers about killing the chickens, so she went along with the joke.

"You're right; I'm not from around here, and my name's Roger, if it's any business of yours." After not talking to anyone for a day Roger kept talking. "I just retired from my job after working thirty-two years and these old bones can't take the cold weather up north any longer. So Judy, Do you like it down here?"

She answered him with. "I've been here now for about three years now. Are you a snow bird or are you going to be a full time? By looking at the way you're dressed, I'd say you're a snow bird." Normally she wouldn't talk that much to a stranger she just met. Roger couldn't believe his own ear's when she said, "I was married to a S.O.B. that liked hitting women, so when I had enough of being hit I moved as far away from that S.O.B. as I could and this is where I wound up."

Roger looked at her; she was a pleasant looking lady that kept her white hair short and was not a bit overweight. He couldn't believe his own ears that she was giving him all this information about herself. Then he asked her. "Is the food any good here?"

"It's okay, nothing fancy; that's how he keeps the price down."

After talking with Judy, for about a half hour Alice brought Roger his hamburger and beer. He asked her if he could buy her a drink.

"Yea, why not, I don't have anything else to do the rest of the day. What are you eating? You just killed your first chicken, that's what you should be chowing down on; you didn't kill a cow did you?"

For the next couple of hours, Roger and Judy had a friendly conversation. "If you're planning to live down here, there's one thing you have to remember. You're not up north, so get used to doing thing on Florida time. You'll find out that we do things just a little slower down here."

"Hey Judy, since you're from around here, are there any nice hotels close by or someplace I can stay?" Roger asked her.

She told him about this place to go and said, "Make sure you tell the clerk that Flip Flop Judy, that's me, sent you, and he'll take good care of you."

Roger smiled at Judy then said, "thank you; Judy, I sure hope I see you again." Then he got up and left.

Three hours later, he was back at the Bar and Grill. He noticed that all the tables were full; and was about ready to leave when he heard a familiar voice, "Hey Chicken Killer, come on over here; we won't bite you for Christ sakes."

Roger knew whose voice that was, and made his way over to the table. He nodded at the other couple that was sitting with Judy.

"Judy told me a lot about you." Gary said.

"I hope it wasn't all bad." Roger told him.

"So you got a chicken on your first day here, that's something to be proud of. By the way I'm Gary and this is Sally my better half. Sit down, and take a load off. How long are you planning on staying down here?" Gary asked him.

"I don't know yet; it depends on a lot of things. Can I buy you a drink, Gary? You too Sally, You already know that I had a free drink today. By the way, what was the waitress name again?"

"Hey Alice, we need a drink before our fish over here runs away," Judy said laughingly.

"Walks away; remember, we're on Florida time now," Roger said, but before Florida time could kick in, she was asking what they wanted. Alice couldn't afford to work on Florida time, not when she worked for tips.

When it came to Roger he said, "A Bud Lite and some chicken nuggets this time."

Everyone got a laugh out of that, and Judy said "You remembered. You might make it after all." Then she asked him if her buddy over at the hotel fix him up?

"Everything worked out fine. He's a good guy to know." Before Roger finished eating his chicken nuggets, another guy came over and sat down at the table.

"Roger, meet Jim Boy. He's been down here as long as anyone can remember. Where did you say you were from, Jim Boy? It's been so long I forgot." She asked him.

"I'll give you one guess and its God's country." Then he spelled out. "MICHIGAN."

"If I remember, your job went overseas and you got a nice little buyout for your retirement." she said.

"I would have stayed up north but I couldn't take the cold winter weather either."

"Well put it here," Roger said as he offered his hand to Jim Boy. "That's the same reason I came down here, only my company didn't go overseas yet;"

"Knock on wood," Jim Boy said.

"So tell me, how did you find this place?" Roger asked him.

"You won't believe this, but a damn chicken ran out in front of me and when I swerved to miss it, I hit a curb and got a flat tire right out front of hear. That's how I found this place. The last count is, so far I got three chickens." He stayed there drinking and talking for another hour before leaving.

The next morning Roger got up early and left. He was gone for six days before he came back; when Roger returned, the first thing he did the next morning, he went right over to Rogg's Bar and Grill. When he went to the back, he was expecting to see Judy or Gary and his better half Sally, but no one was there; after setting down Alice came out and said, "Well I'll be, it's the chicken killer. Welcome back. So what's it going to be?"

Roger asked her "Where everyone was at?"

"I don't think you met Ann yet. She's one of the groups that hang out here; Her Uncle died three days ago and everyone is at the funeral. By the way, she came from Canada like Gary and Sally did."

CHAPTER 3

"Let me ask you a question, Alice. That's if you have a minute. Do you know where there are any good places to rent or may be to buy down here? You know I think I'm beginning to like this place a little more every day, and wouldn't mind living here. Down here, you guys have that beautiful sunrises and most of the people are friendly and when it rains, the rainbow always ends up in the Keys."

"When the group gets back from the funeral, ask April. She used to sell real estate on the side. I think that her uncle's place will be going on the market pretty soon. But if you want to fit in down here, first you'll have to dump those Yankee clothes. Then go up the street to the thrift store and get yourself something decent"

"Thanks a lot Alice. and I'll take you up on that," he told her.

Alice was a young girl in her twenties. She was a little bit on the thin side, and loved to talk. Her hair hung almost down to her hips, and she had a real southern Florida accent with a small tattoo of a rose on one of her legs and a heart on her arm with a man's name in it. Which probably was her X's; "How long have you been down here?" Roger asked her.

"Oh, about all my life; I was born in Key West and lived most of my life there." she answered Roger. She heard someone inside call out her name, and said, "I've got to go now; but remember, you, "Want to talk to April; she'll set you straight and make sure you get a good price too." After waiting on another customer, Alice returned to where Roger was setting.

Roger asked her "Hey Alice, you wouldn't mind if I asked you another question would you?"

"It depends on what it is, if I'm going to answer it or not, and how big of a tip you're going to leave me," she said smiling.

"You know, you're a pretty girl, so why aren't you married?"

"What makes you think I'm not married?" she said to Roger.

"I'm sorry. I didn't mean to get personal."

"I got married when I lived in Key West. After being married for only ten months, the jerk I was married to didn't come home one night. I ran all around that town for three days and nights before I found out he was gay and ran away with his boyfriend and I never saw him again. I don't know if he is alive or dead. So I guess I'm still married."

There was not very many people over at Rogg's Bar and Grill and no one was sitting at the Tiki Bar. After Alice got caught up with her work inside, she came back and sat down with Roger. "So Chicken Killer, I told you a little bit about me. Now would you like me to tell you a little bit about the others that hang out here?"

"Yea, I wish you would; this should be interesting." Roger told her.

"Well if you don't know by now, April came from California. She lived there all her life, and still loves the place. I'm pretty sure she was a school teacher, and sold houses on the side to make ends meet. She couldn't afford to live in California after she retired. It was so doggone expensive there that she couldn't live the life style she was used to living before her retirement. She looked around like you did, and this is where she ended up, only but she didn't kill a chicken like you did."

"Orders up," someone inside yelled, with a heavy German accent.

"Hold your horses a minute, will you?" Alice yelled back. "That's Kenny the Kraut; He's our new cook. Well I have to go now; but I'll be back in a minute."

Five minutes went by before Alice returned and sat down next to Roger and started talking again, this time it was about Ann. "She came down from Canada about ten years ago, I 'm not sure, but the rumor around here that I heard is she had to leave in a hurry, something to do with her taxes, that's why she never goes back up there. Remember, I'm not sure on any of this so don't tell anyone you got this information from me."

"My lips are sealed," he told her.

"The tall girl is Judy, she's known as Flip Flop Judy; I think you know why she got that nick-name. She is a hard one to figure out; she never said anything to me about her past or where she is from. And no one else will say anything about her either."

Roger didn't tell Alice that Judy had already told him about herself.

Alice kept on talking. "When Gary and Sally lived in Canada, they owned a small Ma and Pa type bar. It was just for the locals, something like this place. It didn't make much money, but it gave them a comfortable life. Then one night a drunk came in with a gun." Kenny the Kraut called before Alice could finish telling Roger about their only son, and why Gary and Sally moved to Florida right after the robbery, and Roger never did fine out what happened. During the next couple of months, Roger found out a lot of interesting things about this group of old people that hung out at Rogg's Bar and Grill, that they normally got together about twice a week and would reminisce about the old times, how some of the time the group was taken advantage of just because they were old, and had white hair. They wouldn't let the younger generation who played the harmless little jokes on them get away with it. But most of the time they just talked about the old times, when they had good bodies without all the aches and pains, They talked about all the latest gossip that was going on around the island, but mostly just enjoying life. It was an easy going life style down here. Especially with this group of friends. You couldn't go a day without seeing a smile on someone's face. Someone once told him that Alice was born in Key West, which he already knew and meant nothing to him. And that she was conceived during Fantasy Fest. And that's the reason she turned out like she did. He found out; that this bunch went on their share of Cruise and Bus Trips. That way, they could drink and party, and not worry about the driving. Roger once put a bumper sticker on his car that read "Spending my kid's inheritance." Which everyone got a kick out of it, and told him, "They would help him spend it if he needed some help doing it.

After Roger was in Florida for a couple of months, and he was pretty sure he was going to stay here. The first thing he did when he got up one morning was, he sold that big "Gas Hog" he brought down from up north and bought a little "Rag Top." He thought that having a convertible it would give him a better chance of meeting and picking up the younger "Ladies." Little did he know that down here in the islands, the older ladies liked "Rag Tops" just as much as the young ones did. The old gals got a kick out of the wind blowing though their white hair; it made them feel young again and full of life. After a year and a half of driving in this stop and go traffic during the peak season, he picked himself up a second hand golf cart to drive around in, especially when the "snow birds" **were here. This way he was able drive on the** side of the road to get around all the stop and go traffic. He could even drive on some lawns when the traffic was real bad, when he had to go back and forth to Rogg's Bar and Grill. At times it was a job in itself.

Roger went with April to see her uncle's house. The place was just over 850 sq. ft. and stood on posts 6 ft. off the ground. By looking at it, it would take a little elbow grease to get it back into good living condition, and then you'd have a decent looking place to live. The house looked like a little cottage, which it was made for. If Roger bought this place, he'd paint it light green with pink and blue trim. So after a little bickering back and forth with April, he got the house at a fair price. Now he could park his golf cart and the rag top under it. While he was painting his new house, all his new free loading friends came over every day to watch him paint and drink his beer.

One night when everyone was enjoying their beer and wine, laughing and enjoying the warm evening air Roger said out of the clear blue sky, "I've noticed that you're limping again, Sally. Do you know that out of the seven of us, we've had nine new knees and four new hips. Isn't that a crock of shit?"

Sally said back to him, "That's a lot of operations. They say getting old is supposed to be The Golden Years of your life."

Roger answered her. "Yea that is if you're a Doctor."

"You've got that right," Sally said;

"None of us could make it through the Airport without getting patted down first." Judy said after cutting in. "Some of those TSA officers aren't all that bad looking either. If they wanted to pat me down, I wouldn't try to stop them."

Then Sally finishes what she was saying. "I know. I'm not going to let another saw bone cut on me as long as I am able to stand this pain and can stand up."

"If you're having too much pain, don't wait too long honey or you might hurt something else," Ann said to her friend.

Jim Boy just sat there and listened to the whole conversation, without saying a word, when Sally finished talking, he said, "Do you believe in reincarnation Sally? I do, and I think I'd like to come back as a cute little puppy so everyone would rub my belly. No, let me take that back, I think I would like to come back as a gorgeous women, that way all you guys would fight over me, just to see who would buy me a drink, or maybe a Rock Star."

"Stop it, Jim Boy, just stop it" Sally said. "Why don't you come back as one of them damn chicken's, so we can run over your ass, then you'll shut up." Everyone at the table started to giggle and say right on Sally.

"That's not very nice Sally." Jim Boy told her.

"Well knock it off and drink your beer, you're getting on my nerves", she told him.

"I think he's just having one of those senior moments", Roger said, but everyone knew what he was talking about.

"That reminds me," Sally said. "Gary and I have our yearly physicals coming up in a couple of weeks."

"Don't remind me." Gary told his wife. "Every time I see a doctor he gives me so many shots, he must think I'm a pin cushion or something, and then he preaches that I should lose another ten pounds."

"You'd feel a hell of a lot better if you did," April said. "Try to smile and be happy Gary, that will help," "Nothing can help when you get half dozen shots." He told her. Just then they heard the cluck, cluck clucking sound coming from around the side of the building. April started to laugh and said "What do I hear Gary?" Then she said "chick, chick, chicken."

"Stop it April, I know for a fact that they use bigger needles on men." For the second time, from around of the building came cluck, cluck again. This time everyone on the patio started to laugh.

When the group didn't play their weekly card game on Wednesday, Jim Boy said, "I can't remember where we played last week. Are we suppose to play over at your place Roger?"

"Yea, it's my turn and I'm pretty sure everyone will be there too. Why, don't you remember? We didn't play last week because it was April's birthday and we had that big surprise party for her," Roger told Jim Boy. "Do you remember now? She's the same age you are now Jim Boy." Roger looked over at him and said. "I'm going home, to rest up for tonight. I'll see you guys at 8 o'clock" he said before he left.

At ten to eight everyone was there, and ready to play. Roger told the group. "Everyone knows where I keep the booze, so help yourself." After everyone got what they were drinking, Roger asked, "What are we playing tonight, Six handed Hand and Foot?"

"Didn't we play that the last time we played? How about Train or something we haven't played in a while," Sally asked.

"Sure, that's okay with me; I'll have to get the game out."

When Roger set up the board game, Jim Boy said, "What are we playing for, I fell lucky tonight?"

"Well Jim Boy that depends on how much you're willing to lose" Ann asked him.

After they played for a little over two hours, and had four rounds of Roger's booze, Jim Boy stood up and said, "Well I'm done, you guys cleaned me out. So I'm going to take off."

"Tell me Jim Boy, how much did you lose tonight," Gary asked him.

"Just a couple of dollars, that's not too bad."

Gary looked at him and said. "Are you sure it was only a couple of dollars, I think it's more like eight or nine." Gary corrected him.

"That doesn't make any difference, how much I lost, does it? As long as we had fun, that's all that counts." then he walked over to the door and said, "See you guys tomorrow."

"Okay," Sally said. "Drive carefully and thanks for the money."

After Jim boy left, Roger said, "You guys should take it easy on him; I can see he's getting worse every day."

Then Gary said, "He's the one that won't take his medicine." After that everyone said goodbye and went home.

Once again it was a nice sunny day, and the group was having a few drinks over at the Bar and Grill. After Ann had a couple more drinks, she said, "When are we going on another cruise?"

"Are you shitting me" said Sally, "The last time we went on one you were sick most of the time. I can't count the number of times you got sick and lost your stomach on one hand."

"Yea, but this time it will be different. I'm planning on taking Dramamine."

"Yea, whose leg are you trying to pull, we heard that story before. All you want to do is make up for all the fun you missed out on the last time we took a cruise. You remember, don't you? When we were on the cruise to Mexico, You ate crackers while we had lobster,"

"I know what we can do so you don't get sick," April said. "Why don't we take a ride on the Mystery Train this year to see the Christmas Light, That way you won't get seasick."

"You're right, but I remember that the train broke down and we had to take a damn bus all the way back home," Ann said.

"Remember how we couldn't sleep on it all the way home?"

"You bet I do and I remember the time that the three of us went deep sea fishing, and if I remember correctly, you were the one that lost her stomach, so there, Smarty Pants."

"Who wants another drink before they close this dump down?" Sally asked the women.

Roger said "No more for me, I don't want to get sea sick, even if I stay on land. My son and grandkids are coming down tomorrow so I have to clean my place up a little. I hope they'll only be here for a week." He said jokingly.

"I'll knock on wood for that." Jim Boy said.

Roger hit the table top with his knuckles and said. "Let me see, I think my son has two boys and a girl."

"I hope you can remember their names, you dumb, dumb?" April said after finishing off her drink.

Roger scratched the top of his head and said "Let me think for a minute, yah I sure do." Then he put one finger up in the air and said, "First it's Jimmy, he's the oldest," then he put two fingers in the air, "Then came Sammy, she's second in line, and you know she's a girl." then he put all five fingers in the air, and said, "And the last one is Doug, he should be the youngest. So I'll have to mind my P's and Q's" for the next week."

Sally stopped laughing after she took another drink, and said, "You should be happy, your grandkids are coming to see you, you dumb, dumb. I only wish that I had three grandkids that would come and visit me."

Roger looked over to her then said to Sally, "I might just stop and say hi on our way to Key West." Sally was really slurring her words now, so after taking another drink. Roger told her, "Well, you can have mine for a day or two if you want them." He told her as he pushed away from the table and laughed. He knew Sally good enough to know that she wouldn't remember a word that was said by tomorrow.

Sally took one last drink and said "Good night all, I'll come over tomorrow and help you clean up if you need me."

"You'll never get up tomorrow morning, not after all you drank tonight," Roger told her.

Gary was already waiting at the door for his wife, when she said, "I'll come over to see those grandkids of yours while they're here." She said as she stumbled over to the door where Gary caught her just before she fell.

CHAPTER 4

Driving down high way US 1 in his big shiny car was Butch, his wife Mary and their three kids. Jimmy, Sammy and Doug; they were going to Florida so the grandkids could visit their grandfather. After not seeing his father in five years, Butch still felt uncomfortable being around his father, and the children felt the same as their parents.

"I'm not looking toward to this visit," said one of the kids in the back seat.

"I'm not either, but you will try to get along with your grandfather. Do you understand me? It's only going to be for four days, so please try and behave your self's while we're there."

The next day Roger's son, daughter-in-law and the three grandkids, pulled up in their big fancy foreign car. Just by looking at the three kids you could tell that they belonged to his son. The oldest boy, Jimmy was fourteen years old; he was a tall kid with long blond hair and skinny as a tooth pick. Next was the young girl Sammy. Who was twelve, but dressed like she was a twenty-five old. She dressed way too sexy for her age, and Roger couldn't figure out why her parents would let her wear that bright red lip stick, and a blouse that was too small for her. Her parents had lot's money, they could afford to get something that fit properly, and the shorts that girl wore; they were way too short for a girl of her age. And last was the nine year old, Doug. He was just the opposite of his siblings. He wasn't just a little overweight, but way too heavy for a boy of his age. Anyone could see that he never did a days work in his life, or went outside and played ball with the other kids. Roger stood in the doorway as his son Butch got out of his big shiny car; stretched his legs then walked over to his dad. Butch was followed closely by his wife Mary. She was a stunning lady. She wore expensive clothes, only most men would say she was a little on the thin side, but she was okay. She was so pale skinned; you could tell that she never did outside work either. Like working in a flower garden or anything else that was outside. Just by looking at her you knew if she spent more than an hour in this hot Florida sun she would burn to a crisp. Roger stepped off the porch to greet his son with a big hug, but Butch reached out to shake hands. Roger took one look at him and said "What's with the hand shake, I need a hug. It's been way too long, son." He reached around his son and gave him a long hard bear hug. After the hug was over he looked at the pale one and said, "You're next." You could see Mary was very uneasy and would rather not have come. Roger could see she was uncomfortable, so he hugged her just a little longer and harder. When he stopped hugging her, he told Mary that she was as pretty as ever. She backed away from him with an ice cold smile on her face. Then he looked over at the kids and said, "My God, how you kids have grown. Let's go inside, and get out of the sun. I have something for you kids to eat and drink inside." As the kids started to walk to the house, Roger said "Stop, hold it right there, didn't you forget something?" He paused for a minute, and then said, "Your suitcase's, come on, did you forget them or did you expect your mother to carry them in for you?" Roger said with a little smirk on his face. They all stopped and looked at their mother with a blank expression on their face, if you could have read their minds, and knew what they were thinking. It would be something like this "Like what does this old man think we are; his slaves?" Their mother and father both stood there looking at them. After seeing that the kids weren't going to do anything and their mother and father just stood there looking like they were a statue. Roger said. "If you push the button on the tail gate it will open, then you can grab your suit cases. It's not that hard to understand is it?"

The three kids looked at their mother in wonderment, not moving a muscle. "Go ahead children, and do what your grandfather said;"

"After you take yours in, you can come back and get your mother and father's too." Roger wanted to see if the kids could make it up the steps caring a heavy suit case.

"That's Ok Dad, I'll take ours. Now; do as your grandfather said."

Roger's house only had two bedrooms, he planned on sleeping in his room and his son and wife could sleep in the other one. "You boys can sleep on your blowup mattress, and Sammy can sleep on the sofa. Then after you kids rest a little while get cleaned up and we'll go get a bite to eat. Who wants some escargot and raw oysters?" Roger asked them. The three kids looked at their grandpa like "Are you for real, old man," and let out a YUK. Mary, Butch and Roger, just about fell over laughing, After the three of them stopped laughing Mary looked over at Roger and told him "The children weren't used to eating that kind of food. Can they have something else?" She had to turn around so she couldn't see their face to stop laughing.

"That's no problem, Mary." Roger looked at the kids and said, "How would everyone like a Big Mac and some fries for supper?" This time he didn't hear YUK. So off they went to MacDonald's. When they finished eating their Freedom fries and Hamburgers, they all went back home.

As soon as the kids got inside they pulled out their cell phones and flopped down on a chair, so they could play their games. Roger put up with that for about five minutes. He hadn't seen his grandkids in four years and all they wanted to do was play games on their cell phones. No way was that going to happen. "Come on kids, I'm going to teach you a new card game to play, so put your phones away."

Doug looked at his mother and said, "Do we have to?"

"Yes you do, now mind your grandfather and put those phones away." Roger asked Mary. "What'll it be Mary? What do you want to play? Screw Your Neighbor or Hand and Foot?"

While putting their phones away, the kids saw how slowly he moved. Maybe by moving slow, their grandfather wouldn't want to play.

"Well, what's it going to be Mary? You are going to play too, aren't you?" The old man said to her.

"Yes, I think I will. It sounds like fun. Why don't we play Screw Your Neighbor, that one sounds interesting."

"Get over here Butch, you're playing too, and bring some money," he told his son. When everyone there was setting around the table, he began to explain the game to them. "First, everyone get three quarters."

"I don't have any quarter's grandpa." Sammie said looking at her mother.

"Me neither," the other two said.

"Well Butch, you're the banker, so you have to see that each one gets three quarters."

After the family played three games of Screw your Neighbor, Roger stood up and said to the boys, "That's it for tonight, guys. We've got to get a good night's sleep because we're getting up early to go fishing. Remember the early bird gets the biggest fish."

After Roger went to his room, Jimmy looked at Doug and said "Boy I'll sure be glad when we get out of here; who cares about some dumb old fish anyway."

Before the sun even came up the next morning Roger went into the living room where the boys were sleeping and said "Remember what I said about the big fish. Let's go boys, you got ten minutes to get dressed." Fifteen minutes later the two boys came out. When Roger saw how they were dressed, in long pants and a long sleeved shirt. He shook his head and told the boys, "We're going fishing guys, we're not going to church, now go back inside and put on some shorts and a T-shirt. No fish in its right mind is going to bite on a hook if someone is dressed like that."

This time around the boys came out looking like fishermen. They stayed out there fishing for a good hour and a half. Roger had to teach both boys how to put a worm on the hook and he proved to them that it was okay if you got your hands a little dirty. After they caught a fish he showed them how to take a fish off the hook. After the boys had fished for about half an hour, they both knew a little bit about fishing now. Not very much, but now they could do it without his help.

When the fishing slowed down, Jimmy asked his grandfather "I know that you taught my dad how to fish, but why won't he teach us?"

"I wish I knew the answer to that Jimmy, I think he's just too busy with his work, that's something he'll have to answer. But if I were you, I'd keep asking him until he shows you how to fish. You know, he's a pretty good fisherman." After they caught enough fish for dinner, the three fishermen headed in. After they got the boat tied up at the dock, Roger told the boys. "Go tell your mother to fix something for breakfast; I'm going to clean the fish, then I'll be right in." Roger figured it wouldn't do any good if he pushed the boys, to hard right off the bat.

While he was cleaning the fish he could hear Jimmy and Doug telling their mother and father who caught the biggest and most fish. And that it wasn't that bad having to put a slimy worm on the hook. "Grandpa said I can drive the boat the next time we go out." Jimmy told his mother smiling from ear to ear. "I can't wait; I sure hope we go fishing tomorrow. That'll be okay, won't it Mom?"

"We'll have to see what your grandfather has got planned for us first. Now go wash up and get ready for breakfast."

A half hour after the boys had left to go fishing; Sammy had gotten up. Since no one was around to talk to, she got dressed and went outside. Once she made her way to the back yard, she saw one of the wild chickens clucking and running around in the yard. This was something totally new to her; up north they don't have wild chicken running around, she had no idea what she shouldn't do. So she started chasing the bird. She had a lot of fun chasing that old chicken, she ran and ran, and ran after him. Just getting out of the house and running and running, was more fun than playing on her cell phone. Last night, she didn't hear her mother say, "Put your shoes on if you go outside, or your feet will get too big for a young lady." It seemed like her mother never stopped yelling at her. "Be careful so you don't get too dirty." Kids just didn't do this in the big city where she lived. Mary had just about finished cooking breakfast when Sammy came running in and told her Mother, "Momma look at my legs, they itch real bad. I think something is wrong with them, I'm getting lots of little bump all over my face and legs."

Mary said to her daughter, "Well, stop scratching it," after she looked at all the little white bumps on her legs and face.

"But they itches and hurts so much, I can't stop." Sammy said to her mother. By then the men and boys had come into the kitchen for breakfast. When Roger saw Sammy's leg, he knew what she had gotten into.

Mary looked at Roger and said, "Do you think we should take her to the emergency room?" She looked over at Sammy and said. "I told you to stop scratching, now stop it." She gave her daughter a stern look and said, "What'd you do, eat something you weren't suppose too."

Roger bent down on one knee to have a better look at it. Then he asked Sammy. "Did you go out in the back yard, honey?"

"Yea" she said with a tear running down her check. "I saw a chicken and was chasing it."

"That's okay. Did you go into some bushes that have little white berries on them?"

"Yea, that's where the chicken went, how did you know?"

"I know a lot honey; you didn't eat any of the berries did you?"

"No" she said looking at the floor.

"Don't worry, you didn't do anything wrong. I think you just ran through some Poison Ivy, that's all." Looking over at his son, Roger said "Go to the bathroom medicine cabinet and get me that little gray bottle on the top shelf." Then looking back at Sammy, he said, "We'll get you fixed up in no time at all, sweetheart. I don't think we'll have to cut off your leg or arm either." he said with a smile on his face, but remember honey; you can't scratch it, Okay? Or you'll make it worst." He patted her on the head and said, "You're Okay. Did you get that old chicken?" he asked as he rubbed on some of the gray lotion that was in the medicine cabinet.

After everyone ate some of Mary's not so famous cooking, they squeezed into Butch's big shiny car and headed off to Key West. After walking around the downtown, and Malory Square. Roger noticed that everyone was having fun and enjoying themselves. Everyone except Mary; she didn't enjoy all that walking. "Come with me Mary, I want to show you something I think you'll like, and don't worrying about the others; they'll be okay without us for a while." After walking another two blocks, Roger told his daughter-in-law, "You're in for a big surprise, Mary. I really think you'll enjoy this place. And you can even sit down if you'd like to."

As soon as they went around the next corner, Mary said, "It's Earnest Hemmingway's house; Can we go inside, and sit for a while? You know I read all his books?" Roger could see the life coming back into her face. If he would let her, she would sit there for the rest of the day. After sitting for only fifteen minutes, he could see that it put her in seventh heaven. Roger told Mary to stay there rest up and he'd be back for her shortly, A half hour later he came back for her and said "I hope you're rested up? I found another place to take you."

"Okay as long as I don't have to walk a mile to get there; I don't see how any place down here can be better than this."

"It's not very far from here,"

"Where are Butch and the kids?"

"There out doing what every tourist does when they come down here. After a short walk, Roger and Mary came to the Mel Fisher's Museum.

"Let's go in." Roger told Mary.

"Why, what's in there?"

"Come on with me, you'll see, I'm sure you'll like it."

"Well Okay," Mary said, wishing that she would have stayed at the Hemmingway house, where she was able set.

Going up the steps, she told Roger. "Maybe I can set for a while once we get in there."

"Come on. It's not that bad, is it?"

"You're not the one in 2 inch heels either." She said.

Once they were inside and Mary saw all the gold, she forgot about sitting and her sore feet.

"Easy Mary, easy does it," Roger jokingly told her.

"I never saw so much gold, is it real?"

"You'd better believe its real, every last ounce."

Roger and Mary spent almost an hour walking around in there, and when they left Mary had filled up a shopping bag with goodies from the Mel Fisher Museum. When they were walking out, Mary looked over at Roger and said, "Thank you so much for bringing me here. Now I hope Butch doesn't get too mad at me for spending so much."

"If he does, just tell him to come and see me, I'll set that young man straight." Roger said, as he smiled at her.

"I think I went a little over board," she said smiling from ear to ear. She said. "I just couldn't stop buying, I just couldn't stop, I don't know what came over me. I just had to have everything I saw, there was so much gold in there. A girl can't think right."

After seeing her smile like that, Roger didn't care what Butch thought, it wasn't his money she was spending, so he didn't care if Butch liked it or not. He made more money than Roger ever made. Butch was making money hand over fist.

After walking two blocks they ran into the group. "Who wants to go to Sloppy Joe's and get a bite to eat?" Roger asked.

"Yea, I do I do." Everyone said in agreement with him.

Walking over to Joe's, Roger saw Mary whisper something in Butch's ear, and all of a sudden Butch turned white as a ghost. Roger knew what Mary just told her husband, and I'll bet it was about how much this trip was going to cost him.

Walking up the steps to Sloppy Joe's, there was a man dressed up like a pirate standing at the top of the stairs with a large Blue and Yellow McCoy, of many colors on his shoulder. The pirate said to Doug as he started to walk up the steps, "ARRR Mate, might you want to pet my little friend?" Looking at the pirate, Doug didn't know what to say or do. So he nodded his head yes, hoping it was the right thing to do.

When Doug started to lift his hand up to pet the McCoy, the pirate said in a very loud voice, "ARRR mate, you have to say ARRR ARRRR first, or he'll take your finger off." Doug froze. He didn't want to lose a finger; he looked over at his mother.

"Go ahead," she said. "It's okay. But remember you have to say ARRR ARRR first."

Doug stopped looking at his mother and looked at the McCoy again, this time he said in a soft voice "ARRRR ARRRRR."

Before he could finish the McCoy said "arrrr arrrr Mate" in a lough bird voice.

"Go ahead mate; say it again, but louder this time," the pirate told Doug.

So Doug said in a loud voice that was almost a scream, "ARRR ARRR",

And the bird repeated right back at him "ARRRR ARRR mate."

And Doug said, "ARRR ARRR" right back at the bird. After three or four ARRR ARRRR's everyone in Sloppy Joes was laughing,

The pirate said, "Okay Okay, that's enough mate, you can pet the bird, but be gentle with my little friend." After petting the bird, Doug was grinning from ear to ear. The pirate said to all the customers in the place, "How about a big hand, for my little buddy here?"

Everyone in the bar applauded, making Doug turned red, and said to his mother, "Mom, let's go."

Mary said to her new little mates. "Okay, but let's get something to eat first, then grandpa wants to take us on a sail boat ride, isn't that going to be fun?"

Once everyone was done eating they all walked down to the pier where the whole family went on a three hour sail boat ride around the island. Butch and Mary went and sat up in the bow of the boat like young lovers. Mary was hanging on to her shopping bag for all she was worth. Jimmy met a young girl that looked almost the same age as he was and made friends with her right away. They were inseparable for the next three hours, her hair was the same length and color as his, and was just as thin as Jimmy. Looking at the both of them from behind, you had a hard time telling one from the other. This had to be a match made only in Key West. They were so thin that Roger had to worry about a big guest of wind blowing them overboard, and they surely didn't want to be around any adults. Roger and the two youngest kids sat all the way in the back of the sailboat, they helped the crew pulling the ropes to raise and lower the sails. After they were out for a half hour Roger pointed to the water and said, "Look over there, did you see those two dolphin jumping out of the water?" Just then three more dolphins broke water.

"Look, look. Did you see them grandpa?" the kids were yelling. "Look over there, there's another one." yelled the kids again. For the duration of the sailboat ride, Sammy and Doug had the time of their lives; they helped pulling the ropes and watched the dolphins. Sammy's itching had eased up so she wasn't too uncomfortable now.

When the Windjammer pulled back into the dock, Roger asked "Did everyone have a good time today?" Butch and Mary just smiled; you knew they had one of the best days they had in a long time. Sammy and Doug said they sure did have a good time, and wanted to do it again. Saying it was one of the best times they ever had. This was the first time they had ever been on a sail boat, and the first time they saw a dolphin jump out of the water like they just saw. This was by far the best time they had in a long time. Roger knew that the two youngest ones never set sails before, and would have a lot of fun telling their friends about it when they got home. Even after the boat was tied up at the dock, Jimmy kept trying to get the phone number and address of the girl he met, but with no luck.

After showing him what to do the next day, Roger let Jimmy take the boat out by himself; it was only a small fifteen foot aluminum boat with a ten horsepower motor. But to Jimmy it was a three point racing hydroplane with a fifty horsepower Mercury on the back. Jimmy had the boat out for three hours before it ran out of gas, racing up and down the shore, and jumping over his own wave. Later that day, all the guys went down to the water's edge to skip stones, Mary would stay up at the house so she could lay in the hot Florida Sun, she wanted to get a tan before they left. It would only take two or three hours to change that pearly white skin she had into a rosy red sun-burn. At the beginning Mary thought it looked neat to be that red. Roger warned her over and over about getting too much sun and told her to be sure she put some Aloe on her skin before she got burned up. But at the time being red as a lobster and going home with a tan was more important. She wanted to get a good tan before they left for home, so she could show her friends up north.

Down at the beach, Roger said to the kids, "I bet I can skip my stone more times than you can." The kids looked at their grandfather and wondered what he was talking about. An old man could never outdo them anyway. The kids heard about this stone skipping, but never tried it. So after looking at the kids, and knowing that they didn't know what to do, Roger picked up a flat rock and gave it a toss, it skipped on the water four times, "See, there's nothing to it." So Jimmy bent down and picked up a round rock and gave it a toss, but his didn't skip once. It hit the water and sank to the bottom of the ocean. Sammy was next and her rock did the same as her brother, and landed on the bottom of the ocean without a single skip; "Come on over here," Roger said to the kids "First you have to find a stone that's flat on one side and round on the other, then you put your first finger around it likes this." He gave each one a stone that would skip, and then he showed them what he was talking about. "Then with your hip and wrist you throw it like this. And it'll skip every time." Once the kids learned what too do they had lots of fun skipping stones. Some of them even skipped 7 or 8 times. When their dad saw how much fun they were having he joined in. After Doug was skipping stones from the shore, he took off his sandals and waded up to his knees into the water, he was looking for the perfect stones to skip. After looking for five minutes he found a shiny one and showed it to his son. Roger took a look at it and said "That's a Petoskey stone son. They're found only in one place, and that's up in Michigan. Someone must have brought it down here and lost it. There's an old Indian legend about finding a Petoskey stone, but I'll be darned, I forgot what it was. Well finders keepers, you got yourself a souvenir son". When everyone got up the next morning; Roger took all of them out to breakfast, that way Mary could take it easy with the sunburn she got yesterday.

On the way home Roger had his son stop at the Marina, and asked who wanted to learn how to scuba dive. Now they knew why there grandfather made them bring their swim suits. Walking into the office he told the kids to do everything Captain Sam told them to do. The captain was a man about five feet five, going bald on the top of his head, and was working on a good sized beer belly. "You'll have a lot of fun with him." Roger told the kids, and then he gave Captain Sam his phone number and told him they would be back later to pick up the kids. "We'll be at my house if you need anything." Roger, his son and his wife spent the next four hours sitting around the beach enjoying the peace and quit. When the men drove in the parking lot later to pick up the kids, they all came running out of the office to the car, trying to talk at the same time. All of them said what a wonderful time they had, and how Captain Sam was a cool guy and taught them how to scuba dive. Then Captain Sam took them out in the boat, and had them dive in eight to ten feet of water, and got to keep all the lobsters they caught. Altogether the three of them caught six lobsters. That would be one for each person.

At suppertime that night Roger got out his big black kettle and started a fire on the beach. When the water was hot he put in the potatoes, sausage, and the corn. Mary and Butch knew what they were having for super. "Well, it looks like we'll have the fresh lobsters that you caught today for dinner tonight." The kids were so excited they still hadn't stopped talking. Roger said it was okay to let them play down by the water until it was time to eat their freshly caught lobsters.

When it was time to put the live lobsters and clam's in the boiling water. The two youngest ones wanted to set them free. Only after Roger explained that's how it's done, the kids helped him throw everything in the pot. After eating all they could, everyone sat on the beach and watched the sun as it set over the water, then everyone played Screw your Neighbor, and not once that night did the kids ask to play with their cell phones. The next day they packed their suitcases and loaded them into the car without having to be told to do so. Mary tried cooking one of her not so famous breakfast again, nothing fancy, but it was a good one for her cooking skills.

While Rogers's son and family were down here, Jimmy met a girl on a sail boat ride, but was unable to get her phone number, and got to drive his grandfather's boat. That really made his trip super; Sammy found out the hard way that you can't chase chickens in the woods wearing shorts without getting posing ivy. She had the time of her life skipping stones, she said that one of them event skipped ten times, and couldn't believe how much fun you could have at a Clam Bake. Doug wasn't afraid to put a worm on his hook or take the fish off the hook no matter how much it was wiggling, that is if you were lucky enough to catch one. When he goes back to school, he can tell all his friends how he went scuba diving, and cough a live lobster with his hands. What can I say about Mary, other than the sun-burn, she has enough gold for the rest of her life? And his son Butch has a happy family, what else could one ask for. Driving up Highway 1, on their way home Roger could see the kids sticking their hands out the car window waving good bye as the car drove out of sight. One of the kids in the back seat said to his dad. "I hope the next time we come down here; we get to stay longer than three days,"

Sammy put in her two cents also with, "And we don't have to wait four years before seeing grandpa again. He wasn't all that bad after all." Everyone in the car agreed with that.

After Doug and his family left to go home, Roger went over to Rogg's Bar and Grill. He was surprise to hear that "Sally had fallen and broke her arm the night before Roger's family came down. She was so drunk when she left Rogg's she tried kicking one of the wild chickens that run around in the parking lot and tripped over her own feet and fell. After that, Gary took her home and she fell again trying to go up her front stairs, that's where she broke it. Since then Gary cut her off all of her boozes. You know she's not a happy camper right now, so when you see her be careful what you say around her and please don't say anything about the chicken or draw a chicken on her cast. That is, if you want to live, you know what I mean."

"Is that all that happened when I was gone?" Roger asked.

"No, Jim Boy had another one of his dreams while you were gone. This time it was about an all-black wedding, and he was the only white person there. The best part about this is. He was the one getting married." "You're right, that is hard to believe. It looks like the snow birds are coming down here earlier this year." Roger said as he took another drink of his morning coffee.

CHAPTER 5

One night, Roger and Gary were sitting in one of the local a bar's; without anyone else. They were having a couple of drinks and just having a good old time by themselves. Both of the guys were singing and laughing. After ordering another drink Roger told Gary, "Do you remember that Gold Digger that tried to get her hooks into Jim Boy?"

"You bet I do, she wasn't all that bad looking for someone that was supposed to be 60 years old."

"I wonder what Jim Boy said to her that turned her off so fast."

"I don't know, but then she tried getting her hooks into you, after Jim Boy dumped her."

"I know, but once when I figured what she was after, I got all I could get from her. Then I asked her for a loan to help me get by until I get my next check because I was living on social security and. Boy did she ever hit the road fast."

Michigan State just won the National Championship, and both Roger and Gary had their green and white T-shirt on. The funny thing about that was, neither one was from Michigan, or went to Michigan State. They were laughing and singing the Michigan fight song, only Michigan State won. They were buying drinks for everyone in the bar, even the losers that were setting at the bar, and man oh man there were a lot of poor losers in there this night. There must have been double the number of snow birds that are normally there, and most of them didn't like Michigan. Some of the guys in there wouldn't take the drinks, others turned them down when they found out it was coming from a Michigan fan, even when it was free. One of the guys told the bartender "to stick the drinks up our asses if we sent anymore over there."

At about nine o'clock Gary said "he had to go home; Sally wanted to get up early for some unknown reason." On the way out Gary stopped at the table where the sore looser were setting and said "Go Green." He didn't expect them to say "Go White" back to him; instead they said "Fuck you ass hole." Gary knew what that meant so without saying another word he left, and now poor Roger was sitting there all by himself.

One of the losers got up and walked over to his table and said, "Hey jack ass, take this," and gave Roger the finger, then threw the remaining glass of beer in his face.

After wiping most of the beer off his face, Roger said, "What's the problem mister? It's all in fun."

The drunk bent close, to about six inches from Roger's face and said. "I think Michigan stinks, I think Michigan State stinks, and I think people from Michigan stink. So what do you think about that?" By then his two buddies had staggered over to the table.

Roger looked up at the drunks and said, "I don't want any trouble guys. So why don't you go back to your table and we'll forget this happen."

The two drunks that staggered over said to their buddy "Come on, Mike, it's not worth it, he's just an old man that has nothing else to, and our beer is getting warm."

When the three men turned around and went back to their table. Roger was still sitting at his table and said at the top of his voice, like a dumb ass, "Hey all you jack asses, Go Green and stick this up your ass." He gave them the bird and started to laugh. By then, everyone in the bar was looking over at him, knowing that something was going to happen. It took about one second for the three drunks to stumble back to his table and another second and a half before Roger hit the floor. Every time he tried getting up, one of the sore loser drunks knotted him back down. All the guys at the bar began to chuckle, they knew he drank too many beers and couldn't help himself; there was no way he could stand up by himself. Once he almost got up, and they hit him a couple more times, and down he went. When he was on the floor he noticed a pair of muscular black arms punching one of the drunken snow birds that didn't like Michigan or Roger. It took the black man only two more good hits and all three of them jackasses took off. They didn't even stay around to finish their beers. Out the front door they ran with their tails between their legs. If Roger had one ounce of energy left, he would have said, "Go Green." To the three drunks as they ran out, but he couldn't move or say anything, he drank too many beers with Gary. While he was lying on the floor the same pair of black arms that just saved him reached down and helped him get up, "Holy Shit," Roger said, "If it isn't Clyde. I thought I left you off somewhere in Georgia."

"You did my friend; it took me five years, but I found you like I said I would. It looks like every time we meet, one of us is getting our asses kicked." Roger wasn't able to get a word in. Clyde continued. "Do you remember me telling you about my sister Tisha. Well she lives about ten miles south of here and I'm going to be in her wedding in three weeks. What was all this all about? Why did they jump you?"

Before Clyde could say anymore, Roger said. "They were just some snow birds that are poor losers. No one likes to have fun anymore."

"Yea, I know, I stopped to have a drink and I saw this dude standing over someone; I'm sorry buddy, I didn't know it was you or I would have been here quicker. When I looked the second time I saw all three of them, and they didn't look too happy. That's when I recognized you, and figured I'd better stick around just in case you needed a little backup, I didn't forget how you saved my ass in Tennessee."

"Yea, wasn't that something how we kicked their asses? We made those rednecks run like hell."

"Yea, but we were younger then."

"So this is where you live now. I've been through here a couple of times, I've been thinking about you buddy, but I never thought we'd meet like this."

"So your sister is getting married. How long are you planning on staying down here?"

"That's up in the air. Remember, that's the same thing you said to me."

"I hope you'll stay here long enough to meet some of my friends. I think you'd like them, and yes, they like to drink. They're not sore losers like those three jack asses."

"I'd like that, and don't you plan anything during the third week of July; I'm counting on you going to my sister's wedding."

"You know Clyde; I think I'd like that very much. So what are you drinking?" Roger asked. "Hey bartender, we need a round over here." Looking over at Clyde, Roger said, "Buddy, after living down here as long as I have, these old bones still ache."

"For an old fart you handled yourself pretty good."

"What you just saw was the beer talking." After having two more drinks, Clyde said he had to go, and the bartender said Roger had enough and wouldn't serve him anymore. As the two guys were walking out of the bar, Roger said to his friend. "I'd love to go to Tisha, wedding." When they walked around the corner of the bar to the parking lot, Roger yelled out. "Holy shit, someone picked my golf cart up and wedged it between those two trees again, I'll bet you anything it was those damn snow birds."

Clyde just about rolled on the ground laughing, when he saw that. So he told Roger "I'll take you home and we'll get it out tomorrow, but please old buddy, don't bring it to the wedding."

During the following week Roger told his friends what happened at the bar and how someone put his golf cart in between the two trees again, and everyone was invited to the wedding in three weeks. Jim Boy said "You know that's only a week before we take the bus up to Miami to watch the ponies run."

"So that's no problem; just don't lose all your money at the track this time."

The next week, five of them went to Miami to see the horses run. It was pretty uneventful except some scam artist tried to take Gary's money. He said he had the winning ticket, and was in a hurry and that he didn't have to time to cash it in, if Gary would give him a hundred bucks he would give him the ticket worth five hundred dollars. Other than that there was no big winner on this trip, but no one lost his shirt either.

The day of the wedding, came before you knew it. The weather turned out to be normal. Another day in Florida with lots of sun, so Roger decided it was okay to put the top down on his rag top. He remembered that Clyde said he didn't want him to bring the golf cart. On the day of the wedding, only the three men decided to go, Roger, Jim Boy, and Gary. The girls stayed home that night. It seemed like they already had something planned for that night, so it was no Biggy, they'd be the ones that were going to miss out on all the drinking and dancing. Everyone knew Roger loved to dance, for an old guy like him he was pretty good. He knew he was going to have a good time. And since this was a black couple's wedding, he wouldn't be going home hungry. There'd be all kinds of soul food there. Like baby back ribs, greens, ham hocks and plenty of other comfort foods. The three guys jumped in the convertible and off they went to the wedding. When they pulled into the parking lot, five big black guys all dressed in black and wearing white turbine wrapped around their head came running out. As soon as Jim Boy saw them come running out to the car, he broke out in a sweat. He was having a flash back to the dream he had earlier, when he was the only white guy at an all-black wedding, and he was the groom. They looked mean as hell. As soon as Roger pulled in the driveway and parked the car, the five black men surrounded the little car so it couldn't back up or go forward, with-out hitting one of them. What the hell is going on? Roger thought this must be some kind of a joke or something? Then he saw Clyde come out with a big smile on his face, and he knew it was a joke. With a serious look on his face, Clyde opened Rogers's door and told him to get out, now Clyde knew he wouldn't take off.

Looking over at the biggest guy with his arms crossed, he told him, "Search them for weapons."

"Yes Sir."

When all the black guys stopped laughing, Clyde introduced his brothers from their Brotherhood. He was still having a hard time trying not to laugh, and then he began to introduce the brothers.

"This is our Imperial Wizard, El Julian," Roger just looked at El Julian and gave him a little nod. "Next to him in line is the Grand Pupa, Zed Isaiah, and the First Lt. is James, and next to him is the Secretary of Arms, Brother Willard." He was the biggest guy there, "He's the one you want if you have any trouble, but I know you won't, not here, not tonight." Clyde said. "I know you won't remember their names, but if anyone gives any of you guys some trouble, get a hold of me or one of these guys." When Gary and Jim Boy knew it was safe, they got out of the car and looked at one another, the five black men started pulling the turbines off their heads. All five guys started smiling, and just about fell on the ground laughing again. Roger and his friends still didn't know what to think of this; he tried figuring out what kind of trouble he got his friends into this time. Should they try to run or stay and fight? He just didn't know what to do or what was going to happen, so they just stood there looking at one another. When the laughing stopped, Clyde said. "If you could have seen your faces, you turned whiter than a white man; it was worth a million bucks buddy."

"You mean we're not going to die tonight?" Gary said in a low voice,

"No. Not tonight. We're just having some fun with you guys; we do this with all you white folk that come here for the first time." When Clyde stopped giggling he said to his friend. "Come on buddy, I want you to meet my sister." Looking over at Gary and Jim Boy, he said. "You guys can go get your self-something to eat and drink.

Inside the Church/Hall were about eighty to a hundred people, all dressed in their best Sunday going to Church clothes. Looking around, Jim Boy saw they weren't the only white people there, making him feel better.

"There she is, over there talking with those women" Clyde said pointing at a middle aged woman; dressed in an ivory colored suit with ten to fifteen other ladies gathered around her. "Hey sis; this is the guy I was telling you about."

She extended her hand to him and said with a warm smile, "Any friend of Clyde's is welcomed."

"It's a pleasure to meet you, Tisha,"

She answered him with "So you're the Roger that Clyde has told me about. Feel free to eat anything and make yourself at home. And I apology for what my brain dead brother did outside. Especially, since you kept him from getting his butt beat in Tennessee."

"That wasn't a problem Tisha, and I'm glad to meet you also. By the way, you're a very lovely bride."

"What a gentleman you are, thank you again". The rest of the night went by uneventfully. The guys had plenty to eat and drink, Gary and Jim Boy tried dancing with some the girls. But most of the young ladies there didn't want to have anything to do with an old white man. When the wedding reception was over and everyone was walking out to their cars, Clyde caught up with his friend and jokingly said, "Hey buddy, I have an extra turbine if you want to join the Brotherhood, you could be the first white boy to join?" "Thanks buddy, but I'll have to pass on that one," Roger told Clyde.

"Well, Ok, but you can't say I didn't ask you. Good bye and I hope to see you again, only sooner the next time." Clyde said, as Roger climbed into his car. "No more of this five year stuff or my Brother Hood will have to come and get you."

"Take care my friend, I promise it won't be five years before we meet again, and thanks for not bringing that golf cart." Roger waved to his buddy as the rag top pulled out of the parking lot, and the three men headed for home after a night of having fun, trying to dance a little soul, and eating too much food. A night they'd not likely to forget very soon.

CHAPTER 6

When Alice brought Roger his drink, he said to her. "You know Alice, when I got up this morning I had nothing to do and when I go to bed tonight I still won't have anything to do."

Alice set his cup of coffee down and said, "Well, knock yourself out mister. Grab a rag and help me wipe off some tables. I don't want to hear you cry, about not having anything to do. It's the 4th of July and it's going to get busy pretty soon."

After Roger wiped off the three tables, he called Alice over before the group came in and said, "I can't complain anymore about not having anything to do."

It was the 4th of July. And most of the group was at Rogg's Bar and Grill by then having their morning drinks on cleanly wiped tables. It was another typical day in

Florida. The temperature was still in the 90's at 5 o'clock. There wasn't any breeze coming off the ocean, so it wasn't going to cool off outside.

April asked. "Who wants to go down to the beach and watch the fireworks later on?"

Right away Roger said, "No, once you've seen one, you've seen them, they are all the same."

Gary and Judy said, "There would be too much traffic on the road for us, because we can't see well enough to drive at night."

So the three girls decided to go by themselves. April, Judy and Ann said they wanted to go even if none of the guys went. Judy said, "It'll be nice to have the girls go without you guys for a change. We can take a blanket and lie on the beach and have our self's a few drinks. I think it'll be fun."

"Me too", Ann said,

"I'll pick you guys up at 7 o'clock so we can get a good spot to watch the fireworks."

When they pulled into the parking lot, just about every spot was already taken. "Wow, I didn't think it was going to be this crowed," Ann said

"Over there's one." April pointed. After parking the car, the girls got their blanket and cooler and went down to the beach, only to find out that when they got there it was just about completely filled up.

"Over there." Judy pointed. "It's not the best spot, but we should be able to see Okay." As the girls were spreading out their blanket, April was the first to notice that right next to them were five guys sitting in beach chairs, and without any women. Once the girls had a few drinks and were sitting on the blanket, they began to giggle and talk about the guys sitting next to them.

"Boy what I could do with him, the one sitting closest to me." April laughed.

Then Ann said "I'd let the one next to him keep his shoes under my bed any day."

Judy wouldn't be out done and told the girls. "Well I'm not picky, I'll let any one or all three of them put sun tan lotion on my back." While the girls were giggling and laughing, they noticed that the guys were checking them out too. When the one that April thought was a hunk, made eye contact with her, He had a big smile on his face, and raised his drink to toast to her. Shortly after that toast, it was dark enough for the fireworks to start. When the first one went off everyone started clapping and cheering. April took another look at the guy she had eyes for, and sure as seeing fireworks on the 4th of July. He was still looking at her. Judy looked over at Ann and said, "Oh, oh. I think she's going to get in trouble tonight." Everyone watched the sky as it turned red, white and blue for about five minutes. April smiled and raised her drink to toast to her new hunk, than she finished off her whole glass. "Easy girl. We have a long way to go," one of the girls said.

April's hunk stood up with his drink in one hand and the chair in the other and walked over to her. "Do you mind if I sit over here?"

"Go ahead, it's a free country, the last time I checked." she said.

Everyone on the beach started to cheer and clap. "Wow, boy oh boy, look at that one." Everyone on the beach was saying, as the largest one of the night went off.

"This is a big blanket and we have a lot of room on it." Before April could finish saying what she wanted to, her hunk jumped out of his chair and lay on the blanket next to her.

Judy looked at April's new friend said to him as she giggled, "Tell your buddies we don't bite." That's all she had to say, all the guys came running over with their beer in one hand and stretched out on the blanket. "How long are you guys staying down here?" Judy asked one of the guys.

"Oh, about four or five days, we came down to do some deep sea fishing."

"For, four or five days, I'll drink to that," Ann said, then the girls chug-a-lugged another drink. The guys wouldn't be out done by the girls and did the same with their beers.

For the next hour and a half, it seemed like the girls were putting a drink down every 15 minutes. When the final finally came, April was out cold. She couldn't remember anything. Her good looking hunk was gone, and she missed out again. The next morning when April woke up in Judy's spare bed, and said. "Oh my aching head. What happened to me?"

"I see you came back to life" Judy told her.

"What happened, why am I over here?"

"You don't remember, do you? Last night you drank enough to float a battle ship."

"Oh my God, do I need a cup of coffee or something."

"It's just about ready; you don't remember anything about last night, do you?"

"All I remember is us girls going to watch the fire-works at the beach, that's about all."

"Can you remember making out with that big hunk of a man on the blanket?"

"You're joking with me now, was he good looking? She asked. Tell me. Did I, or didn't I?"

"You didn't," Judy said. "Wait a minute; and I'll tell you more, I think the coffee is ready." As Judy was walking out to the kitchen she said, "You would have, but we stopped you, because there were eight of us on one blanket." Before Judy got back with her coffee, April had passed out again.

CHAPTER 7

A week after going to Miami, the group was sitting out back on the patio having a few drinks, when Gary said, "its quiet around here."

"What do you mean by Quit?"

"You guys went to that wedding just two weeks, ago, didn't you?" April said,

Then her friend Ann said. "From what I heard you had a good time there and you had a little run in with the Brother Hood."

"It wasn't too bad; they didn't scare me at all. And yes, we had a few laughs," Roger said.

Jim Boy butted in, "Remember when the black guys came out dressed like they were members of some Brother Hood or something.

"That's what I just said Jim Boy. Gary and I thought we were goners, and I almost wet my pants. I was so scared;"

Gary answered Jim Boy with "You'll never forget something like that as long as you live. You know? To me, this year seems like it's going by slow. I know we have, but it seem like we haven't done anything lately."

"Does anyone know what happened to Flip Flop Judy? I haven't seen her in three or four days now." Roger asked.

"It's not like her to stay away that long."

Ann looked at Roger with a straight face and said, "I thought you knew. Her only son was killed last Monday."

"O My God, I didn't know. Why, what happened?"

"Well what I heard was, he was in a small convenient store and got shot during a robbery. That's all I heard; I don't know how true it is. We'll just have to wait till she comes back."

"That's terrible. Your kids aren't supposed to die before you do, I hope they catch whoever did it, and put him behind bars for the rest of their life" Roger said,

"Do you think we should take up a collection for flowers or something?" Sally said as she already had tears running down her cheeks.

"That's already been taken care of," Ann mentioned quietly.

"You know, that ticks me off." came out of Gary's mouth, which wasn't smiling, and was getting mad as hell. You could see he had a difficult time by him saying a lot of four letter words. "You can't even go to a store for something without taken a chance that you'll get your head blown off. What's this damned world coming to?" You knew that Gary was upset, he was turning red and talking very laud.

"Yeah" said Ann, "What in the world is going on?"

Roger looked over to the counter and said, "Alice, we need more coffee over here when you get some time." Before he could say anything else, from around the corner of the building everyone could hear the chickens clucking. That was a sure sign someone was coming.

Ann spoke up, "You know, we're all a little down, so why don't we just go home and tomorrow, we'll talk about going to Disney or someplace when we all feel a little better."

Roger looked back at Alice, and said "Forget the drinks." The next day, Gary and Sally were feeling a little better. Everyone else was sitting around the table, when Ann said, "Why don't we make planes to go to Disney or someplace fun for a few days? When Judy comes back, that'll help lift her spirits a little, and I know it will help us.

"If I remember, when I first met you guys I killed one of those chickens, and was called the Chicken Killer."

"You know, there'll be a lot of walking if we go to Disney, and we're all in our 60's and 70's." Sally said as she was looking over the table at Roger.

Then Gary said to the group "Everything is made for the young people; if I had a ton of money I'd make an amusement park just for us old farts with gray hair, and wouldn't let any young ones in."

"What if you're bald and don't have any hair?" Jim Boy said.

"Smart Ass, there's one in every crowd, then you'd have to buy a gray wig."

"I'd drink to that if I had a beer. How can you drink to anything with coffee?" Gary said. Just then the waitress came out with everyone's coffee, and Gary said, "I'll drink to that with my coffee,"

"I don't like talking about someone behind their back," Jim Boy said after taking another puff on his cigarette, "But have you seen the inside of Judy's house lately? I think she's turning into a pack rat. She can't go past a damn garage sale without stopping."

"Come on Jim Boy, I see her place every week and it isn't that bad," Sally said.

"Well, if we go up to Disney, we'll have to tell her we're leaving a day before we go, and she can't stop at any garage sales on the way up there to buy more junk."

Gary said "She's one of them lucky people who buy a painting for five bucks and a week later finds out it's worth ten million."

"If that ever happens, you'd better believe I'd help her spend it." Sally told them. Everyone chuckled and said "Yea, me to,"

"So what do you say? Do we take another cruise, or go to Disney. There isn't that much walking on a ship," Judy spoke up. The chickens stopped clucking, so they knew that no one was coming. Someone must have just turned around in the parking lot.

Gary said, "Sally has been bugging me about going on one again."

"Ann said that she would go, if we were going to take a cruise; Roger said "Count me in to. This will be my first one."

"Well," April said. "I might as well go along to, it's no fun sitting around here all day long while you guys go and have all the fun."

"Why don't we make plans to go in maybe four weeks?" Then she said "Who wants to take a four day or seven day cruise?"

"It doesn't make any difference to me, but since this is Rogers first one, how about a four day one." Ann said.

Before the group left for the night, they decided they would take a four day cruise.

Four weeks later, only five people were on their way to Miami for the cruise. Jim Boy had to see his doctor so he told the group to go without him, and he'd go on the next one. Judy wasn't over the death of her son yet, so she passed. This time, they made sure that Ann took her Dramamine, so she'd be able to enjoy this cruise. When they got to the ship it was already loading. So the group boarded without any wait and got settled in, they all met at the pool where April said, "The first Bahama Momma is on me. It's party times guys." They sat there for an hour watching the other passengers come aboard the ship. They got a kick out of watching the first timers. They looked at everything on the ship as they boarded, with smiles on their faces; The ship left the port of Miami at 1600 hours. (That's 4 P.M.)

At dinner, on the first night out Roger said, "Are we going to the Welcome Dance tonight or go see a Broadway Show, or maybe do some Gambling?"

"I don't know what you guys are going to do, but Sally and I are going to play the slot machines, and who knows, we might win enough to pay for our trip," Gary said with his big smile.

"I wouldn't count on that, Gary; be sure you just don't lose your shirts the first night out."

Ann said, "April and I are going dancing, who knows, we might get lucky too, you never know."

"Ha, who in their right mind is going to pickup two old chicks with white and blue hair when all this young stuff is running around here?" Roger said.

"Maybe two old guys with no hair." Ann told him. The two women looked at one another with big smiles on their faces. "I'm going after a rich one with lots of money," Ann said to her friend.

Then April said. "I don't care if he has money or not, I just want a live one if you know what I mean." Ann told her with a smile on her face "Maybe one of us will have to sleep in Roger's room tonight. Because I'm going to dance and dance until the chicken comes home and the sun comes up in the morning. Then who knows, he might even get lucky."

Roger looked over at Gary and Sally and said, "It looks like I'm going with you. These two girls are dreaming already that they'll get lucky tonight, and I don't want to stand in their way."

The next morning when they all met for breakfast, April said "She didn't get lucky, but the guy she danced with most of the night was a lot of fun, he made me laugh and feel good, even if he was shorter than I am,"

"So what about you, Ann? Did you luck out?" Roger asked her.

"No, nothing like April. I think I only danced two or three times all night. I didn't have any luck on the dance floor at all. I almost came over to try my luck on the machines."

"Well it looks like April was the only lucky one last night; One out of five isn't too bad." Gary said.

The ship stopped at port during the night. After they finished eating there breakfast, Sally said, "Let's go on shore and take a sightseeing tour."

"That sounds like it might be fun." Ann said, "Maybe I'll meet a nice single guy."

"Knock it off, Ann, you've got all of us as your friends," Sally told her.

After they finished eating, they all went on shore and took a two hour sightseeing tour. Instead of going back to the ship for lunch, **one of them said they should try some of the local food. Boy that was a mistake; after eating** something that no one knew what it was, and they all got sick before going back to the ship. After seeing the ship's doctor, they all went to their cabins and took a good half hour nap before supper. That day the ship set sail just before dinner and on the dinner menu for tonight was Lobster, which meant Ann was going to eat her first lobster while on her first cruise.

With Ann and April standing at 5' 8" and poor ole Sally was only 5' 3," so no matter how high her heels were, it wouldn't make any difference; she would always looked like the shortest one. Since this was the night everyone was supposed to get dressed up for dinner, the other two girls wore their highest heels, trying to impress any eligible gentlemen, and making Sally look even that much shorter. The five of them sat at the table having a drink before dinner was served. The three ladies were comparing how the other women were dressed as they came in. Some of them were dressed to the Ten's and others looked like they bought there at the Five and Ten, the girls made sure and pointed them out.

They sat at a table that was arranged to seat ten so they had to share the table with five other people who were a lot younger than they were, and just barely old enough to drink, they were putting the drinks down as fast as the group was.

"You'll have to excuse my friends, one of the young guy said, they just got married this past weekend and still think they're at the reception," the youngest one said.

Gary raised his glass to toast the newly married couple; and said "That's no problem at all; we all went thought it our self, many a year ago." Gary told the young man.

Sally started to giggle and said, "This is going to be Ann's first time she has lobster on a ship."

"Hug" The young guy said, looking over at Ann.

"It's a personal joke, don't think anything about it."

When they finished eating their lobster Roger told Ann, "I'm going with you tonight; I have to see this guy April is interested in."

"I think we'll go too." Gary said, "You never know when you need back-up."

"Let's all meet at about 9 P.M. over at the Dance Hall."

"That's Okay with me." Ann said. Then the two girls went back to their room and put on their sexist dresses again, they put their hair up on top of their heads and put on new lipstick, they put on the most expensive perfume they owned.

April went to the closet and came out with a pair of three inch heels. "What do you think of these?" She asked Ann.

"That'll make you almost a foot taller than Kevin."

"I know, he told me he likes taller woman. You know where his head will be when we're dancing, don't you?"

"I sure do, you thought of everything you devil. This'll only be the second time I saw you in that high of a heel."

"I don't wear them very often, you know that."

"Well let's hope the both of us get lucky tonight." As 9 o'clock got nearer, April put on her heels and the girls left for the dance. Going early like they did, they were able to get a good table, right next to the dance floor where they could see everyone and everything that was going on. After Roger consumed a few drinks he asked Ann to dance with him. Gary and Sally also went out to dance; now if Kevin was there, he could see that April was by herself. When the dance was over, and they returned to their seats, April was still sitting there all by herself,

"What's wrong honey? How come the jerk didn't come over?"

"I don't know. I saw him out there with some other women. I could care less if he dances with me or not." Anyone could tell she was unset. "I'm not going to let that little runt upset my trip."

Two dances later, Roger looked over at April and said, "Come on baby, let's shake a leg and make this guy see what he's missing out on."

Halfway through the dance April said, "Look over there, by the bar, that's him, the little guy with the bow tie."

"What do you say we make him jealous?" Roger whispered in her ear.

"Why not?" it's my turn to get even she said, "He knows I'm here and he didn't even bother to come over and say hi or anything." The two danced over to where Kevin was and started to dance cheek to cheek and belly to belly, showing Kevin what he was missing out on.

After setting out the next two or three songs, April kicked off her heels and said, "To hell with him, I'm not waiting any longer, come on Ann, dance with me." So the two girls danced by them self the rest of the night, not once that night did a guy ask one of the girls to dance. That's how that night went. Once again the girls struck-out, neither one of them got lucky on night number two.

Walking back to their room that night the girls had to pass the swimming pool and dressing room. When they got to the lady's dressing room, the door opened and out staggered a young little thing with nothing on. She was holding wet paper towels up against her breasts and down between her legs.

She looked at April and Ann then in a squeaky little voice said "I went skinny dipping and forgot where I put my towel and I can't find my swimsuit any ware. The water's real nice, if you're planning on going for a swim." she said.

Both Ann and April could see she had had way too many Bahama Mommas. "I'll take your word on that," Ann said, as to two older women walked back to their cabin.

"You know, I almost took her up on that." April told her best friend.

The next morning everyone met for breakfast, and Ann asked, "What are we going to do today? You know the ship will be at sea for the whole day,"

Sally spoke up, "Why don't we go to the pool before it gets too crowed over there?"

"That's Ok with me," Gary said with his usual smile. I can get caught up on some of my reading." After they finish eating, everyone met at the pool where they stayed for most of the day. After people watching for an hour or so, Ann and April went for their walk around the ship's deck, so they could talk about girl things, and see if there were any prospects available.

Roger, Gary and Sally were having a drink when Kevin came up and introduced himself. "I'm sorry about last night, I though your friend April knew that a shipboard romance is only for one night." Kevin said to the guys.

"She had her heart set on dancing with you at least once. You really hurt her." Sally told him in an unfriendly voice.

"I'm sorry about that, I didn't mean to hurt her, and she seems like a real nice person. If you would, when she comes back, will you tell her that I'm sorry?" Kevin said as he turned and started to walk away, then he stopped and said again, "I'm sorry about last night folks,"

A half hour later April and Ann came back after having their girl to girl talk. All three of them told April what Kevin had said when he came over.

"I hope the jerk falls overboard in her normal voice." she then said. "Did we tell you what we ran into on the way back to our cabin last night?" April asked.

"No, you didn't say a word about last night. Why, what happened? Did you girls get lucky or something?" Roger laughed.

"Well, when we were walking back to our room, we had to walk past the lady's changing room and we ran into this young girl that was drunk out of her mind. She didn't have any clothes on, just a couple wet paper towels stuck to her tits, and she told us she couldn't remember where she put her towel and swimsuit. Then she wanted to know if we wanted to go skinny dipping with her." We made sure she got back to her room, then we continued back to ours, and no, we didn't go skinny dipping with her. We politely declined her."

"Hell, why didn't you call me? I was in the mood to go skinny dipping last night." Roger said.

"Believe me; she was way too young for you, she was young enough to be jail bait. I'll point her out if I ever see her again." After reading and taking about nothing for an hour, Ann said to Roger, "Why don't we jump in?"

"If you do, I will," he answered her.

"Ok, let's go, on the count of three," Roger slowly counted, "One, two, three." The two got up and ran over to the pool and jumped in. After they were in the water, the other three saw how much fun they were having, then jumped in too.

After a little horseplay and floating around, April said "Look over there, it's our skinny dipper. Only she has a suit on now, and she looks like she is sober too," that caught every ones attention.

Roger took a good long look at the skinny dipper and said, "You're right, I think she is jail bait. Not bad looking though, but she is definitely jail bait." April only stayed in the pool for ten minutes then she got out. She went over to their spot and started to put on some sun tan lotion.

From behind her she heard a familiar voice say, "Can I help you with that?"

She turned around not believing what she had just heard. And there was Kevin. "What?" she said.

"Can I help you?" He asked again, "I'm sorry if I made you think we were a couple the other night."

"Are you for real? You made a fool out of me, in front of my friends, how do you think I should feel? I'm not seventeen anymore. So get the hell out of here, and leave me alone."

Roger and Gary saw what was going on, so they got out of the pool and walked over to her. "Is everything Okay, April?" Roger wanted to know.

"Yea, this ass hole was just leaving."

As soon as she said that, Gary stepped in between her and that the ass hole. Then he said, "Good-by, Mister." Kevin didn't say a word; he just turned around and left, and April went back to putting on the sun tan lotion by her self.

You could tell she was angry, real angry when she said in a loud voice, "Where's the waiter? I need a drink." They stayed by the pool drinking Bahama Momma's until dinner time.

When the group went to supper that night, they were already halfway to the moon. After finishing another fabulous meal, they all of them went over and played BINGO for the rest of the night. Once again, there were no winners in the group.

Little did they know that the ship was running into a depression. This ship was large enough that the Captain wasn't worried. He had been through depressions before and nothing happened, but this time would be different. By midnight the depression was upgraded to a Level One Hurricane, so to be on the safe side. The Captain ordered that everything should be fastened down, and buttons all the hatches; they were still planning on riding it out. At 0300 Hours (3 A.M.) the Captain got a call from the engine room that he didn't want to hear, there was a small fire down below and the ship would be losing all of its power for a half hour, in order to put the fire out and repair the damages. Before the power went out the Captain had the First Mate make sure that everyone had their life jackets ready and for them to stay in their cabins. Once again, the Captain told all the passengers, "There's nothing to worry about. This ship is seaworthy and everything will be okay, it is going to rock back and forth a little when the power goes out, but that also is normal," then repeated himself, "There is nothing to worry about." Little did the passengers know that when the power goes off they'd be at the mercy of the sea without the stabilzers. For the next hour the ship rocked and rolled, it went from side to side, up and down and back and forth, meanwhile, back in the cabin poor Ann thought she was going to die. That damn Dramamine wasn't working as it was supposed to.

"Try looking out at the horizon," April said, "That's supposed to help."

"I can't even see the damn horizon it's so dark out there."

"Oh, okay, well try lying down in your bed and I'll get you a bucket and some wet towels." April said, only by then, it was too late, before she got the bucket over to Ann, she lost her stomach. Everything came up. Everything she ate at supper last night. It went over everything in the cabin. For the next hour she was in pure misery. Nothing the girls tried would work. The ships doctor gave her and a hundred others passengers another shot. But that didn't seem to work either. Poor Ann would just have to ride it out the best she could. Once the ship's power came back on and the stabilizer started working again, the ship became steady again. But by then it was too late; everything in the cabin was dirty beyond belief. The only thing the girls could do now was sit out on the main deck with just about everyone else. The ship was making a straight line for Miami, and it should be back in port within three hours. But it was too late; she had already lost her stomach.

"No matter what they offer me," Ann said to her shipmate buddy. "This is the last God damn time in my life I'll ever go on a damn cruise again.

On the long three hour drive home everyone had something to say; mostly about the ships ride and how it broke down during the hurricane. April was the one that did most of the talking. She talked about the first night at sea when she had that encountered Kevin on the dance floor, and what a fool he made of her. At the end, they all came to the same conclusion, the next time they will know better than to take a cruise at this time of the year. But they all had fun, and everything turned out okay in the long run. When they got home, the next day they all met at "Rogg's Bar and Grill" for their morning cup of coffee. Alice knew what everyone drank and already had the first set-up waiting for them when they came in. Flip Flop Judy was doing better now and Jim Boys doctor appointment turned out okay. Everyone wanted to hear how their trip went, after hearing about the hurricane and fire from the nightly NEWS. The group sat there for hours drinking and shooting the B.S. They told Judy and Jim Boy everything that happened on this trip. How Ann got seasick, and April almost getting lucky. Gary didn't lose all his money on the slot machines, and Roger, well, he had eyes for a young girl that could have been jail bait girl. He said he went along for the ride, and this being his first cruise, it was one he would never forget, and maybe he might even think about taking another one.

CHAPTER 8

The group sat at their table for almost two hours, only Roger never showed up. It wasn't like him to miss out on his morning coffee. "Do you think he was in an accident last night or did something else happen to him?" Judy asked.

"No, I don't." Jim Boy said. "I think he might have gotten lucky last night."

"He's too old for that." Gary said.

"I don't know about that." Ann said. "I'm not saying we did anything, but I'll bet he's still able to do it."

"Yea, maybe in his dreams." Gary answered.

"Well, I think he got up early and he's off fishing someplace or he found himself a good woman last night, Jim Boy said.

When Alice came over to the table and wanted to know "who wanted a warm-up?"

Sally asked her. "Did Roger say anything about not coming in today?"

"I take it you haven't heard yet. Last night three snow birds came in with all kinds of money to spend, and were buying drinks for everyone. And knowing our Roger, he wouldn't turn a free drink down. After four drinks they asked him to come over and join them. It was two men and one woman Roger thought. For being down here on vacation, they sure were dressed up awful nice, but he didn't paid any attention to that. Every so often, I saw the women put her hand on Rogers's leg and try to put the make on him." Jim Boy was beginning to pay attention now. "I really don't think Roger knew she was a cross dresser."

"You're shitting me," Ann said.

"Not our Roger." April giggled, "He knows more than that."

"When they wanted him to go home with them, I put my foot down and told the three of them "He's with me, and they had better leave now." I said "Key West is an hour south of here, now get going." I had the bartender help me get Roger into my car, and took him over to my place when I got off work."

"Are you talking about the same Roger I know?" Gary asked her."

"Yep, the same guy," she said. "He's probably still sleeping it off on my couch right now."

"I can't believe it. I've seen him get high many times, but never anything like what you just described, I wonder if they slipped a pill into one of his drinks." Flip Flop Judy told her.

"Wow, I can't get over him not knowing she or he was a cross dresser. He must have done a pretty good job dressing up or Roger was totally out of it," April said.

Then Jim Boy butted in. "Darn, I wish I would have stayed here last night."

"Jim Boy, you wouldn't have known what to do if you every ran into one."

"I know a lot more than you think I do, one of these days I just might show you."

April started to laugh and said. "Wait till I see him. He's never going to live this down."

CHAPTER 9

Roger and Gary were sitting at Rogg's one evening watching two little Geckos playing tag on the trees that surround the patio. Every once in a while a cool ocean breeze would blow through and cool them off. Roger looked at Gary and asked him. "What are your plans regarding the hurricane that was coming our way?"

"You know, if it doesn't change direction it's supposed to be here in four days, and you know we can't wait until the last minute to leave, because I-75 well be a big parking lot by then."

"So, what do you think?"

"I thinking we should get the hell out of here no later than noon tomorrow, or like you said we'll get tied up in all the traffic."

"What do you think, should we take two or three cars?"

"I'm thinking two cars should do it. Shouldn't that be enough?"

"I think so too, three in my car and four in yours."

"Okay. Make sure you gas up today and take enough money and clothes for at least five days, and be sure your shutters are up. And tell the women we are leaving at ten, that way they might be ready by noon."

Roger and Gary finished there drinks while watching the two Geckos play before going home. The next day all seven were at Gary and Sally's place ready to go. The two guys that were driving went over the plans one last time and then said, as they walked out the door. "I'll see you in either Naples or Miami." When the hurricane went up the Gulf side of the state, they met in Miami and had a four day long party. After the storm blew over, they headed home. For the next two days, the only thing you saw on T.V. was the damage that was caused by the hurricane. If anyone that lived down here didn't have gray hair before listening to the nightly news, they did now. When they were halfway down the chain of Island, the State Police stopped them at a road block and said; "There was so much damage, only permanent residents are being allowed beyond this point." After hearing that kind of news from the police, if your hair wasn't already white, it surely would turn white now. A half hour after they got past the State Police check point, a large black car tried to get through the same check point, but didn't have the right papers and was turned around. When they had about two more hours of driving ahead of them before they got home, they started to see some of the damage that happened. Large trees were down across the roads, some houses had the roofs blown off, and damage was everywhere. All the power lines were down, there were no road sign's left up, and you had to know how to get home by using landmarks. The closer they got to their homes, the more the girls started to cry. Roger had Ann and Flip Flop Judy with him in his car. The closer he got to their place, the more Judy began crying uncontrollably.

"What am I going to do now, oh Lord, please God, please don't let it be mine, I don't know what I am going to do, it's just one terrible thing after another. First my son, now my house. Please God have mercy on me" When they finally got to Judy's house, you could see that both of the girls little cabins were unlivable. After they looked around for a half hour, they went over to Roger's. Since his house was built on stilts it didn't have any water damage inside. Only a couple roofing shingles were blown off, but the place was livable. He didn't have any water or electric, but it was dry. The two girls took one bedroom and Roger had the other.

An hour later, Gary pulled up, and sure enough all seven would be staying in Roger's little house. When Roger asked Gary how badly he got hit, he said "I lost part of my roof and a couple windows. I think I'll be able to move back in, if you help me put a blue canvas on the roof, I think it should be livable again."

"You know I'll help you, you don't even have to ask. How bad did the others get hit?" Roger asked, "What about Jim Boys?"

"The road over to Jim Boy's was closed and April had some damage, I think we can get her back into her place in a day or two." But it wound up taking two weeks before April got back home. Ann and Judy stayed with Roger until their insurance money came in. Then, the girls bought a mobile home together. After weeks of looking for his golf cart, which he never found, Roger wound up buying another one. Judy and Ann each got a golf cart to use until they got back on their feet too.

For two weeks after the hurricane, no one saw or hear any birds or saw the little geckos that played all day. One thing no one missed was the clucking of the local chickens, no one knew where they went, but all of them came back three weeks after the big storm.

Rogg's Bar and Grill lost the outside Tiki Hut Bar and some tables, and were able to open the place back up in two days, using propane and a power generator. No way the people living on the island had a place to come and get a warm meal.

CHAPTER 10

The long hot summer was just about over, and the snow birds were returning. That was the main conversation this morning; everyone had something to say about how the traffic was getting so horrendous. Then out of the clear blue sky Jim Boy said "Hey, why don't we go down to October Fest this year? As long as I've lived here, I never went there for October Fest. I hear it's really a blast at this time of the year. Some of the stories I've heard about what goes on down there would make your hair curly. Isn't that right Ann?"

"This hair turned curly long before I moved down here smart ass, and it's never been to a Fantasy Fest." She said.

"So what do you think? Should we make plans to go **down there or not? What do you say?" Jim Boy had to say.**

Ann then said, "Let's take a vote?"

"You know I'm voting yes." Jim Boy said, who is the first one to vote most of the time.

"Count me in too." was Rogers vote. He'd never been there either, and just wanted to see it, and if it is as good as everyone said it is. He couldn't believe everything he heard, and that it was as wild as everyone said.

"Well hell," Judy said, "I'm not getting any younger and who knows how much longer this body will last so I'm vote number three for yes."

"Come on," Sally said to Gary, "I think it will be a lot of fun. We can get painted up and everything. Doesn't it sound like fun to you?"

Gary had to stop and look at everyone before he said. "Well, I'll go, but you're not painting me up."

"I can imagine how you would look all painted up and running around half naked," Jim Boy said.

Gary had a smile on his face, and then told the group "Okay, count us in." After Gary said he was going.

Ann said, "Well, me too. It might be fun, so I'm in too"

Flip Flop Judy said, "Since Alice use to live down there. Shouldn't we ask her too?"

"Yea, good thinking Judy," Ann said. "She should know her way around Key West pretty good."

The next time Alice came out, Ann called out, "Hey Alice, come over here, I want to ask to you something."

"Give me a minute," she answered back to Ann. About five minutes later she came back out, and asked "What can I get you guys?"

"Nothing," Ann said. "We're planning on going down to Fantasy fast this year, and since you used to live down there, we thought you'd like to go with us. It's only going to be for a day or two."

Alice didn't have to think about it at all and said, "I'd love to, but first I have to see if I can get the time off." She started off walking back to the cafe, but was running when she got to the building. She ran inside and was back out in less than a minute. (She's not on Florida time now.) Alice said, "Sure, I didn't have any problem getting the time off. I just told Kenny the Kraut I wanted that week-end off or I would quit. So when are we going?"

During the upcoming weeks they had a lot of planning to do. They had to figure out who wanted to strip down and get their bodies painted, and what design would be painted on them, and most important, who would do the painting. This is ware Alice came in real handy, she knew all kinds of people who would do it. If they took the the biggest car, they would only have to take one car down there, and where would they stay if they spent the night. Alice told them "I talked to my Ma and she said she would be happy if we'd stay with her. That is if we wanted to. But we'll have to bring something to sleep on, like sleeping bags or a blow up mattress."

When the day finely came, they all squeezed into one car and headed south to Key West. It was only a two hour drive, so they left on the morning of the big party. They went directly to where Alice's mother lived. After they unloaded the car and got settled in. Jim Boy said "Who wants to go downtown now and see what is happening before it gets too crowded? Or who wants to save up their energy and wait till tonight? I don't know about the rest of you guys but I know I'm not waiting till tonight," Jim Boy said. "I'll be back in plenty of time to get made up for tonight."

"I'm going to stay here and rest up for now," Roger said. The three girls said they would go with Jim Boy and check out the town.

"Gary and I are going to stay here. He's too tired after driving down here. Why don't you guys go and have some fun; we'll get everything set up for tonight."

"How about you Alice?" April asked.

"I'm staying here, I've seen it before, and besides I can visit with my mother now. I'll go tonight."

Jim Boy and the three girls bid them, "Good bye." and took off; they'd been to Key West before, but not to Fantasy Fest.

Going out the door Sally said, "Try not to get into too much trouble." A little after 3 P.M. the three of them came back; they all had a smile on their faces.

April said, "You can't believe what is going on, the streets are already blocked off and lots of the people are getting painted right now."

"Man olé man, I couldn't believe it. It's still light out and some are naked already. I can't imagine what it's going to be like tonight." Ann said,

"You guys haven't seen anything yet; wait until it gets dark out, that's when it'll blow your mind." Alice told them.

"I already know what I'm dressing as" Jim Boy said, he was one extremely happy guy, and was having a hard time keeping himself under control. He wasn't gay, but sometimes he acted like it. After Alice's mother made some hamburgers and hot dogs for the group of party goers, it was time for them to start dressing or getting painted. Alice's mother really turned out to be a big help. Since she lived here all her life, she knew a lot and had everything they needed.

Sally was going to be a sexy police woman and Gary would be her prisoner. Roger didn't know what he wanted to be yet so he wore plain shorts and a t-shirt. The two other girls were going with the paint. April, the tallest one wanted to be painted all over in eye balls, eye balls in the front, back, the tits, legs and everywhere else, even her private parts, big eye balls and little ones, lot of eyes, from the top of her head all the way down to her toes. Ann was doing the same, only she wanted to be an Indian, so she had feathers painted all over her body, just like April was doing with her eye balls. Then came Jim Boy. He was going as a cross dresser. Lots of April's and Ann's clothes fit him and he could wear the heels April had for the cruise. They were just about his size, and Alice's mother had a wig for him to wear, then he put on some red lipstick. He could pass for a lady of the night, anytime, day or night. Alice got painted up like a nurse, she'd done it before, and so it was nothing new to her. Judy wasn't over her son's untimely death yet, so she went along only as there care taker. If someone had too much to drink, Judy would look after them. After walking up and down the streets of Key West for an hour, everyone was checking out what the other party animals were doing, along the way they had consumed a couple of drinks. The women begin to loosen up and started to act silly, since that was what they went down there for. Never before did they run around in the nude, with just eye balls and feathers painted all over them. The reason they went to Key West was. "To Party." Most of the time the women lived a good and health life, they didn't care what anyone thought of them tonight; this was probably going to be their last hurrah anyway, so why not go out with a bang. They were going to have a good time, and that meant drinking, partying, and dancing in the street and maybe getting lucky. Everyone knows that what you do in "Key West, Stays in Key West," especially, during Fantasy Fest. No one knew what was going on with Jim Boy. He would disappear for a half hour, and then he would come back. He was smiling every time he came back, and seemed okay, so it was no big deal. The girls forgot that they were in their 60's and 70's with artificial knees and hips, and couldn't do what a 30 or 40 year old person can do. If they were at home at this time, they would have probably already been in bed.

After Alice was downtown with the group for half an hour, she ran into some of her old school friends that she hadn't seen in a long time, after talking with her friends she told Roger "Tell my mother that I'm with Barb and Sue and not to worry if I don't come home, I haven't seen them in a long time and have a lot to talk about." Like Mother, Like Daughter, Roger thought. This is where Alice's life began, and she definitely knows what life is all about down here.

Gary and Sally saw Ann and April get wild before, but never like this. It seemed every time a good looking guy would walk by, the girls would gang up on him. They tried talking the guys into buying them drinks, and dancing in the street with both of them at the same time. Ann and April were drinking anything they could get their hands on and anything in between that had alcohol in it. Once they accidentally spilled a drink on a good looking dude as he walked by. He was painted up and you just knew he was a party animal by the smile on his face. For some reason the girls went out of their minds over this guy, and tried to lick the spilled liquid off him. He let them go so far before stopping them, when the girls told this guy he could lick their feathers and eye balls off, he wouldn't oblige them for that either. The girls couldn't get any takers. No matter how drunk the people walking by were, no one in their right mind wanted to lick the feathers or eye balls off a 60 something year old woman. Just looking at the grin on Gary's face, he would have given anything if he could join Ann and April, but Sally wouldn't have any of that. Every once in a while Roger would grab a girl walking down the street and spin her around, trying to do a little two step with her. The group just can't keep up with the young people anymore. They were just too old now. No one could get over how Jim Boy was in seventh heaven, one minute he was trying to put the make on a man walking by, than the next minute it would be a woman. Roger was getting higher and higher as the night went on, everyone who walked past him could see he was just a harmless old man that drank way too much and should be back home in bed, that was probably the reason he had no luck either.

Around midnight the group made their way back to the house, where Alice's mother had hot coffee waiting for them. "Well, how did everyone like it? Was it as good as you though it would be or was it better?" They all tried talking at once; just by listening to them, she knew they had a good time and might come back next year. "It looks like we're one short," Mrs. Acton said.

"Alice told me to tell you she ran into Barb and Sue, and not to worry." Roger told her. After a few cups of coffee, non-stop talking and laughing, everyone hit the sack. Between 9:30 and 10:00 o'clock the next morning everyone was up and drinking coffee as fast as Mrs. Acton could make it. But there was no Alice; she didn't come home last night.

Mrs. Acton didn't seem to worry too much, and then told Roger. "She's with her best friend." At 11:00 AM, in stumbled Alice, still in her nurse's outfit.

"I'm sorry; I forgot what time it was. I see everyone is about ready to go, so Mom, I love you, and I'll see you real soon." Alice told her mother.

Walking out, everyone in the group said, "Good by" to Mrs. Acton and told her what a wonderful time they had and they couldn't have done it without her help. Only one person slept all the way back, and by looking at the grin on Alice's face, she probably had the best time of all.

While they were in Key West the big black car that was looking for Roger stopped at Shorty's Motel on Marathon Island, the stranger from the big black car asked for a room for two days. "You're in luck mister. We just had a cancellation. You know every room down here is booked up a year in advance for this October Fest." The person in the big black car thanked the bell hop, and drove down to Key West the following day. After seeing what October Fest was like; he turned around left all the islands after spending only fifteen minutes in Key West.

CHAPTER 11

"Did you guys ever think about getting yourself a golf cart like I did?" Roger said to his friends. "I did once." Gary told him. "But my old lady asked what would happen if I got hit by one of them snow birds? She's not ready to be single yet."

"Tell her, not to think like that. When it's your time to go there's nothing you can do to stop it."

"That's easy for you to say, you're not married to Sally." It wasn't raining very hard, just hard enough to spoil the day. On days like this they'd meet at noon for a couple drinks at their favorite watering hole.

This day Sally said. "Did anyone see Ann lately?" Just then Alice came out and wanted to know what everyone wanted to drink. "Coffee for me," Sally said.

"Me too," Roger said. "It's too early for me to drink."

Jim Boy repeated his order for the second time. "Make my coffee black and hot, hot, hot. You know how I like it." Lately he's been so forgetful and now repeats himself all the time. The rest of the group ordered their usual drinks. For the past week now everyone's been talking about the snow birds and all the chickens that been running around in the parking lot.

A half hour later, Ann pulled up in her car and said. "Sorry guys, I drove past that new Dollar Store up the road and there were no other cars there, so I had to stop."

"I'll bet every Dollar Store in Florida knows you by your first name as much as you stop at them," Roger said looking over at Ann, After taking another drink of his coffee, he said "The way you just pulled into the parking lot, I thought you were trying to get one of those chickens. There's way too many of them running around now, we'll have to do something pretty soon, maybe we can set some traps out or something." He said before taking another drink.

"Well, it never hurts to get a free drink around here," April said.

The rain had stopped when Alice came out with another round of drinks. "Be careful Jim Boy, it's hot." Alice said as she put the coffee cups down. Jim Boy had to excuse himself, and then took off in a flash to the bathroom. He started out walking fast, but ended up running.

Once Jim Boy was inside Gary said to everyone, "I think he's losing it awful fast now."

"Yea, I noticed it too." April said. "Once you start getting Alzheimer's, there's nothing you can do."

"You're right; he should see a doctor pretty soon. He might be able to slow it down or do something for him," Sally said as she started to stand up.

When Jim Boy came back, the rain had completely stopped. Roger stood up and said "Well guys, I'm out of here. I've got an appointment with a big hungry fish that's waiting for me to catch."

"I wish you'd get that fish pretty soon, so you'll stop talking about it all the time, and kill one of those damn chicken on your way out too, like Ann tried to get earlier." That was the first thing Flip Flop Judy had said since she got there. When Roger pulled out of the parking lot, in his little rag top, he spun the tires like he was trying to get one of the chickens.

Sally looked over at Judy and asked, "What's wrong, honey? It's not like you to be this quiet?"

She looked over at Sally and shook her head no, back and forth three or four times. By then she had tears running down her checks. "I'm scared Sally, really scared. When I was taking my shower last night, I felt three lumps in my left breast, that's two more than I had the last time I checked, I'm really scared, I don't know what to do, I can't eat or sleep anymore. I can't do anything. I've been to the doctor a half dozen times now, and they say the same thing every time. I'm really scared Sally. If only you knew?"

Sally got up and walked around the table to Judy. She bent down and gave her a big hug and said, "Try not to worry honey; we'll work this out together. Please try not to worry your head off;" then she gave her another hug. "I promise you that all of us will be here for you through the whole thing."

"I know you will, I went to my doctor and he said that the cancer has spread throughout most of my body now, and you know what that means, it's a death sentence."

"Oh honey," April said, then she paused for a minute. "I'm taking you to see my doctor."

"No, it's no use April; my doctors did everything that is possible. I saw two other doctors; one was all the way up in Miami."

"Why didn't you tell someone sooner? You can't go through this by yourself." Ann told her.

"I know, but I didn't want to be a bother."

"Oh brother, you know we're all family here, you know that you're part of our family." Ann said.

"I know, Yea but." She sat there and didn't say a word. Sally sat next to her in shock; neither one was moving. She knew what was going to happen. That's the same way her mother died.

It had quit raining some time ago when Judy stood up and said, "I'm not feeling too good right now. I think I'm going to go home. I'll see you guys later."

"I'm going with you Judy; you can't be by yourself."

"No, please don't Sally, I'll be okay."

"If you're sure, but if you need anything at all please call me."

"I will, I promise;" Judy told her, "See everyone later." She said as she got up and walked out to her car.

Sally walked out to Judy's car with her. And when Sally came back, she went over to where Gary was sitting and told him everything that she learned from Judy. After finishing their coffee, Gary and Sally went home.

Three weeks later, everyone in the group except Judy was at Rogg's Bar and Grill having their morning coffee, After trying to call Judy, Sally said, before taking a little sip of hers. "I've got a funny feeling; I think I'm going over to her place to see if she is okay. Do you want to go with me?" she said looking at her husband.

"No, I think I'm going to stay here and finish my coffee. She'll tell you more if I'm not there."

Fifteen minutes passed and neither one came back, Ann quietly said, "I think I'm going over to Judy's too,

I'm beginning to think that Sally was right, I have a funny feeling something isn't right over there."

Ann no sooner stood up when Gary's phone rang and when he answered it, he listened as his wife on the other end said, "She's dead, Gary she's dead," Gary heard over his phone.

"Wait a minute; I'm putting you on the speaker phone so everyone can hear this." When everyone there heard Gary say that, a deadly silence fell over the group. No one said a word; it seemed as though even the chickens stopped clucking. Everyone just sat there looking at Gary. "Okay" he said, "What'd you say?"

"She's dead, when I got over here and she didn't answer the door I used my key to get in and found her lying in bed. I think she took an overdose of sleeping pills."

Gary cut in and told his wife. "Whatever you do, don't touch anything. I'm on my way."

"Okay, but hurry, Will yea?" Gary heard his wife say.

Gary, along with everyone else in the group jumped up and went over to Judy's house; Sally had the front door open when they got there, so everyone went straight to the bedroom where she was laying. "Don't touch anything." Roger said,

"Look over here, these must be the pills she took," Sally said pointing at an empty bottle on the night table.

"Someone call the police, did she ever say if she had a family other than her son that got killed?" Roger asked.

"I don't think so" Ann said.

"Yes, she did. One time I think she said she had a daughter, but that was so long ago, and she never said anything else about her." April told them.

"Look over here." Gary said, "She must have been in the Army or something a long time ago."

"She was but she never talked about that either. That's when she was married to that ass hole that treated her like she was his punching bag." Sally said, "What about her daughter?"

"I don't know. We'll just have to wait and see what the police have to say." Sally told Roger. The group looked around for another fifteen minutes before the State Police came. When they got there the police asked everyone except Sally to wait outside. About an hour later Sally came out and said. "We can go home now. I gave them our phone numbers and they'll let us know what funeral home she'll be at. I also told them she wanted a military funeral, and everything I knew. They said they'll take care of everything."

Roger answered her with, "It'll probably be at Crow Island then, it's the only island large enough to have a funeral home."

"Yea, you're right. Well keep in touch. If you hear anything let me know." Ann said.

"Okay, God, I can't believe she could take her own life. She had so much to live for, what a wonderful person she was." April said.

"God damn it. Why did she have to get cancer? When you have cancer, you just don't think right." Jim Boy had to say.

"Come on Gary, I want to go home." His wife said. During the next two days, the group learned a lot about their dear friend Judy. They learned that she was married, and never got a divorce. She has one daughter that lives out west somewhere but no one knew where or what her name was. She spent twenty-three years in the Army as a nurse, and had two tours of duty in Viet Nam. After they have a small funeral service down here, they'll transfer her body up to Arlington National Cemetery for a full military funeral.

The day of Judy's funeral the whole group went up to the Crow Island Funeral Home, alone with half the people that lived on this little island. The owner of "Rogg's Bar and Grill" shut it down for a day in respect to Judy. Now Alice was able to ride to the funeral with some of Judy's friends. The funeral was respectably good as funerals go, and lasted for forty-five minutes. When the service was over everyone was asked to stand while taps was played. When the trumpet player started, everyone in the funeral home jumped when the first volley of rifles were fired outside. It was part of the 21 gun salute for a military funeral. When the trumpet player finished a solider came in and gave everyone sitting in the front row one of the empty cartages. Driving home from the funeral, the group stopped to get a bite to eat, and talked about their dear friend Judy. "I remember how she loved watching the red sun set, especially when a big brown pelican would fly by," Ann said.

Then April continued by saying, "The best time I think she ever had was when we all went to Miami. In my wildest dream I would never have thought she could drink all the liquor she drank that day. I can't see how she made it back to her house in one peace."

"The thing that I remember about her," Roger said, "My first day, when we were sitting on the patio, how she put me through the third degree, she wanted to know everything there was about me. I can't imagine what would have happened to us if she didn't go to Key West to watch over us at Fansty Fest?"

For the next hour everyone had something to say about their friend, Flip Flop Judy. If it was something happy, or something sad, it didn't make any difference, just as long as they said something.

CHAPTER 12

Roger was out back cleaning the small fish he just caught. When Gary drove up, after looking at Roger's catch, he said "Didn't do too good again, huh."

"Not this time, but one of these days I will, I promise you that when I do get him, we're going to have one hell of a fish fry."

"Hey Roger, if you're not doing anything tomorrow, what do you say we go play 9 holes of golf if the weather's okay."

"Let me get back with you on that Gary, but I think so. Were you able to get a tee time, or are we going there and hope to get one?"

"I was thinking about that; why don't we just go and try our luck, the snow birds aren't here yet. If you go, it'll be me, you, Jim Boy and Sally. It's not all that busy yet, so maybe we'll be able to go out right away." After Gary left, Roger finished cleaning all his little fish. The next morning it was a nice Sunny Florida day. Lots of sun, warm weather, and no rain in sight. After Gary picked everyone up they headed north to the Crow Island Golf Course. This was the first time since Judy died that both Gary and Sally had that shit eating smile on their faces at the same time. After about a ten minutes wait they got to tee off. Sally was first to go, she played from the forward tee's. (The Lady's Tee) The first hole was a par 5 for the women and a par 4 for the men. On a good day Sally could hit the ball about 110 yards, but it went straight every time, never did it go to the left or the right, it always went right down the middle of the fairway, and this time wasn't any difference. It went straight; straight as an arrow. That's how she got her golfing nickname, "Robin Hood." because her golf balls always went straight, just like Robin Hood shooting his arrows. Some people said she's still using the very first golf ball she bought. After she hit her ball, she looked back and saw that Jim Boy already had his ball tee'd up and was getting ready to hit it, which meant she had better hurry up and get out of his way. "Wait a minute, don't you see I'm still up here," she yelled at Jim Boy?

Then he said. "Well, hurry up; I'm not going to wait all day." Jim Boy could hit the ball farther than anyone in the group, but there's only one problem, fifty per cent of the time they didn't go straight.

Jim Boy tee'd his ball up and was ready to swing when Gary yelled, "FOUR." Before Jim Boy was able to take his swing.

"What'd you do that for, I haven't hit it yet."

"Just practicing Jim Boy, I'm just practicing for later on." Gary said. That way he was giving his wife more time to get out of his way.

When Jim Boy hit his ball, sure enough he hit a hook that went in the fairway next to him. "I'm hitting a mulligan," he said.

"You're not having a mulligan on every hole," Gary told Him."

"You play your way and I'll play my way, we're not playing for money, are we?" he said. Jim Boy's next shot stayed in his fairway and went over 200 yards. Next up was Roger. He took his first swing without practicing or warming up first, and topped the ball; it only went about 10 yards at the most. "I'll bet you want a mulligan?" Jim Boy said.

"No, I'll save it for later. You never know when I'll put one in the water." Last up was Gary. He had a real good first shot for being short and a little overweight. (He was

Fat) It went straight down the middle for about 180 yards, not vary far but it was okay. Since Roger was away, he was first to hit his second shot, this time it was a lot better than his first one and went over 150 yards. Then Sally hit her second shot, and it went just under 100 yards this time. Gary took his turn and hit his second shot. It could be considered a perfect shot, the ball landed on the green, giving Gary a good chance to get an eagle. Jim Boy was next. He hit his ball far enough, but once again it didn't go straight, and the ball landed some 15 yards off the green, on the left side, then Sally took her third shot and this one also was way off the green. Roger did the same with his third short; the only one on the green was Gary.

When Jim Boy took his turn he hit the ball over the green and down the other side. "Damn it, I hit it a little too hard." You could hear him talking to himself. He wasn't very happy; his next shot was a little chip shot that landed about two feet from the hole. He walked over to his ball and picked it up and said, "It's a Give Me."

"No it isn't, we didn't give it to you." Gary said. The other two players then two putted their balls in. That's how the first eight holes went. When they finally came to the ninth hole, Roger added up everyone's score, and told them that only two points separated everyone. When they started off on the ninth hole, Jim Boy thought he was in the lead, and he wanted to stay there, so he tried to make it to the ninth green in one shot, and protect his lead. He swung as hard as he could, and sure enough, the ball hooked. "FOUR" Roger yelled as the ball went on the wrong fairway.

"I'm going to hit a mulligan." he said.

"Oh no, you're not. You're going to play that one right where it landed." Gary told him. You already had four mulligans today, so play it from over there, where you're supposed to." He gave Gary a dirty look, but didn't say anything else. Roger and Gary hit their balls down the center of the fairway, a 160 and 150 yards away from the green. Then Sally hit hers, and you know what I'm going to say, it went straight as an arrow. This time she hit it 110 yards. She was still away, and took her second shot. This one landed 30 yards short of the green. Which should be an easy chip shot for her?

Jim Boy went over to his ball and hit his second shot over the green and into the woods. He got a little hot under the collar when he saw that he didn't have a shot at the green where his ball landed, he went over and picked up his ball and said, "I'm done; it's no fun playing if you can't have any mulligans."

Roger's second shot went into the left sand trap that guards the ninth green. Gary made the green in two. Sally's third shot hit the green and bounced off the back. Roger was up next and took two swings at his ball and couldn't get it out of the sand, so he picked his ball up and said, "I guess I'm finished too."

When Sally got to her ball, she saw that she couldn't play it where it landed, and being tired, she also said, "Well that's it for me, I'm done too."

Gary walked up on the green and two putted his ball into the cup, when he picked his ball up he said, "It looks like I won, no one's left," he said and started to walk off the green. "It's no fun playing by yourself."

Roger never added up the last hole. That way no one knew who won, and there wouldn't be any fighting on the way home. That's the way it went most of the time when they played golf. When they were walking back to the club house to have something to drink and eat, Roger tapped Gary on his arm and said, "Do you want to have some fun?"

"You know I'm always in for fun."

"Well, when we get to the clubhouse, let's tell Jim Boy that he got a hole-in-1. And tell him that since it's his first a hole-in-1 he has to buy the first round. He'll never know the difference."

"Okay, sounds like a lot of fun to me."

"Tell your wife to go along with it, okay?" Gary told Sally what they had planned for Jim Boy, and she said, "It sounds like we're going to have some fun today."

They all sat down once they were inside the club-house. Roger told the waitress that "Jim Boy here just had a hole-in-1 and he's buying."

Jim Boy looked at the guys and said. "Did I really have a hole-in-1? You're not joking with me are you?"

"You sure did, buddy." One of the guys said.

"Hey Sally, I got my first Hole-in-1," Jim Boy said, smiling at her from ear to ear.

"You know what that means don't you?" she said.

"I think so; I have to buy the first round."

"You're right, Jim Boy. Not only the first round, but you have to buy the first round all day, aren't you glad?" she asked him.

"Yea." "Aren't you glad you got your hole-in-1?" Gary said he was going along with what his wife just said. "You know, now you have to buy us the first round all day long."

"That's okay; I finally got my first hole-in-1." After they ate there food and had a drink, Roger told Jim Boy, "You have to pay now buddy, remember that hole-in-1."

"Okay, I had my first hole-in-1 Sally, that's why I'm paying." After Jim Boy paid, the group got up and patted him on the back and said, "Thanks buddy, how's it feel to have your first hole-in-1?" as they walked out. They had to go past four other bars on the way home, and they planned on stopping at all four of them, since Jim Boy thought he had to buy the first round all day. A mile up the road they came to their second bar. Jim Boy and group went in and had a cold beer. When they were ready to leave Gary said to Jim Boy, "Well Mr. Hole-in-1, get your money out."

"Why?"

"You had a hole-in-1, don't you remember?"

"Yea, I remember, I had a hole-in-1 today."

"Come on, Jim Boy; don't tell me you forgot about your first hole-in-1. Or are you trying to get out of paying?"

"No, no, no, I remember, I had a first Hole-in-1." So Jim Boy paid the waitress as the other three silently giggled amongst them, and left. The next bar was just a half mile up the road and the whole scenario started all over again. Bar after bar until they got home. Jim Boy believed he had his first hole-in-1 and had to buy the first drink in each bar. After the last bar, Gary was feeling his oaks a little too much, so he asked if someone wanted to drive the rest of the way home, He didn't expect Jim Boy to say. "He would."

"Okay Jim Boy, but only because you had your first Hole-in-1. Be careful," Gary told him, then gave him the car keys. He only had about a half mile to go, so what could happen.

When they finally got home Jim Boy said, "See, I told you I was a good drive. That's the reason everyone behind us kept honking their horns. They were telling me what a good job I was doing."

Roger looked over at Gary and said, "I don't have the heart to tell him that's not what that meant." Once they were home, they were in no shape to do anything except sleep, which most seniors their ages do if they've been drinking after playing nine holes of golf.

CHAPTER 13

A couple of days after Roger played in the big golf game, he was watching two little geckos play while listening to the chicken clucking out front, he thought he could do some serious business. He packed his fishing pole and tackle box in the back of his golf cart and took off. He could see visions of that big fish biting on his hook already and the fish fry he promised everyone when he gets the big one. He knew that this was going to be the day. The day he finally gets that big one; when he got to his favorite fishing hole he noticed that there was a strange car parked in his spot. At first he paid no attention to it, for all he knew it was just some snow bird trying his skill at fishing. He didn't care as long as they didn't catch his big fish, there were enough little ones for everyone. He did notice that the cars had an out of state license plate, but this time of the year there were a lot of out of state license plates here. When he was walking down to the edge of the water, he noticed some movement in the bushes along the way and strange noise coming from it. "Hey, is anyone in there?" He yelled as he got closer.

"Go away mister, every thing's okay." The voice came from the Busch.

"Are you sure you're okay?"

"Yes, everything is okay."

"Well if everything is okay, I'm going fishing down there. Are you sure I can't help you. I have a lot of time; I can help you if you lost your car keys or something?" Roger just wouldn't quit. He enjoyed playing with the snow birds. No harm in playing with a snow birds mind every once in a while, he thought.

"Why don't you get out of here and go fishing buddy; I hear the big ones are biting."

"Well okay, he paused for a second or two then said. "There's no hanky pankey going on is there?"

"Please mister, I asked you nicely, now go get yourself a fish and there is no hanky pankey going on, as long as you're here."

"Okay, I'll be right down there if you need some help." he said pointing at the water. "Are you sure you're okay? If you want some help just holler?" He said again.

"You don't want to get me angry mister, I said everything was okay, now get the hell out of here and leave us alone."

Roger could tell that the voice in the bush was beginning to get a little bit mad. "If you say so, but remember if you need some help, I'll be fishing right down there." He said again, as he was pointing at the water. When Roger finally walked down to the water he picked a spot on the beach where he could see both the bushes and the water. After fishing for about fifteen minutes he heard sounds coming from the same bush, and then he saw a stranger he never seen before and a young little lady coming out from behind it. She was trying to hide her face so he couldn't see who she was. It almost worked until she tripped over a piece of driftwood and her hands flew up in the air. Then Roger got a good look at her. It was the little bank teller down at the Island Bank; she must be paying dividends to a good customer. It's too bad that I'm not the good customer over at that bank, he thought. The weather was perfect and he had nothing else to do, so he stayed there and fished for another hour. When he went home the big one was still out there somewhere, it got away from him again, but he wouldn't go hungry either, because the little ones he cough taste just as good or better than the big ones.

A week later Roger went to the Island Bank to cash his check, and "Heavens to Betsy" there was the little bank teller. After Roger signed the back of his check he handed it to her, and gave her a little smile and nodded, he didn't want to embarrass her, because someday he might want to become a good customer at this bank, he thanked her after he got his money, and started to walk out, only on the way out he couldn't help himself. He stopped and turned around. Temptation got the best of him and he said to her. "I hope you had a good time the other day."

She didn't say anything at first, but then she replied to that statement with a little grin on her face and said, "Have a nice day sir."

CHAPTER 14

On a rainy day, a large black car pulled into Roger's driveway, and the stranger that was inside got out. He looked all around then walked up to Roger's house, and knocked on his door. When Roger got to the door, he saw a strange man dressed in black. Roger knew he wasn't from around here. People didn't dress that way down here. The guy just stood there looking at him.

"Can I help you?" Roger said. The stranger still didn't say a word, he just looked at him. "Is something wrong?" Roger asked again.

After what seemed like eternity, the stranger that was dressed in black said, "Are you Roger?"

"Yea, I'm Roger, who's asking?"

"Were you in the Air Force in 68 and stationed at Tinker before going to Viet Nam?"

Roger began to wonder where this guy got all this information and what he was up to. "You're right once again mister, and yes, a lot of guys left from there going to Viet Nam, so what is it that you want?"

"Did you know a girl named Sandy, Sandy North? She also was in the Air Force there?"

For a minute Rogers heart stopped beating. "Okay buddy," Roger said staring right into his eyes "What the hell is this all about?" He was getting too personal now, "and you had better be telling me the truth."

"I believe I'm your Son." Rogers's heart just about stopped again, this time he had to take two steps backward and lean against a chair. "I don't want any of your money or anything; I just wanted to know who my father was."

Roger couldn't believe what he just heard. "Come in, come on in." He was at a loss for words and didn't know what to say. He was just hit with a bomb, so he said something dumb, to give his heart time enough to slow down. "Do you want a drink or something?" Roger stopped and scratched his head, while he caught his breath. He sat down and got right back up, then said. "Yea, please take a seat over there. Did I hear you right, did you say you were my son or something like that? I don't know what you're up to, but this had better not be a joke or any funny business. What did you say your name was?"

"Russ, Russell, I go by Russ. I'm sorry I didn't give you some kind of advanced notice. I should have called you first, before hitting you with all this at one time. You were a hard man to find and I didn't know how else to do it."

Before he could say anything else. Roger stopped him from talking and said. "How's your mother? My God man, is she okay? Where does Sandy live now?" Roger just kept asking question after question, he didn't give Russ a chance to answer any of his questions. "My God, I tried to keep in touch with her when I went overseas, but she stopped writing and, and."

This time Russ butted in "I'm not blaming you; there's nothing you could have done. After you went overseas, she got station in Turkey."

"Wait a minute, you mean your mother went to Turkey?"

"Yes, that's what I'm trying to tell you. She didn't know she was pregnant when you went over to Viet Nam. I'll have that drink now, if you don't mind."

"She never told me, she didn't say a word to me about being pregnant. My God man, I would have married your mother in a second." Roger stopped talking and looked at Russ then, he said. "What'd you say you were drinking?"

"Just water. After I grew up she told me how much she loved you, and how she didn't want to ruin your career, that's why she never told you."

Before Russ could finish what he was saying, Roger took over the conversation again. "Where's she's living now? Man, I wish I would have known about this before. How is she, what's she doing now, when can I go see her?"

"I'm sorry to tell you this, but she died five years ago." After hearing that news, his heart just about stopped for good. "She got married right after she returned from Turkey. She got married but it didn't work out, so after three years they separated, and she never remarried. I guess she just couldn't stop loving you."

"Well, how are you? Do you have any brothers or sisters?"

"I'm okay, and yes, I have a son."

"That's nice, real nice, and you have a half-brother too, his name is Butch." Roger told Russ.

"I'm sorry, but this has to be a short visit. I have some business I have to take care of, so I'll have to leave now, but will it be okay if I come over tomorrow? That is if you're free, I'll come over at; let's say 9:00, is that okay?"

"I'll make sure it's okay." Roger said.

"I'll see you at 9 sharp." Russ said, and then left.

"And bring a picture of your mother, if you have one with you.'

After Russ left, Roger said to himself, "Damn it, I didn't get his phone number or where he's living or anything. The kid wanted something to drink and I didn't get him anything. What if something happens before he comes back?" Roger had so much excitement in him; he had to let it out somehow, so he went over to the Rogg's Bar and Grill and told everyone in there what had just happened.

After talking for a half hour, Sally told Roger, "Be careful, you never know when someone will try to steal your money away from you."

"He knew too much about me Sally. I'm positive he was telling me the truth. Who would have known that I left Tinker to go over to Nam in 68 and who else would have known, I loved Sandy"

"Even if you're sure, you still had better have a blood test. If he is your son, he won't mind; so does this mean you'll have to buy more Christmas presents next year?" she said as she was taking another drink.

The next morning when Roger saw the big black car pull into the driveway; He was out the front door and down to Russ's car before he had the car door open. "Come on in, I already have the coffee made. Boy, do we have a lot of catching up to do. I'm sorry I didn't get you your water yesterday." Roger just wouldn't stop talking. "I hope you brought some pictures of your son and mother, if you had any. Come in, come on in and I'll show you some pictures of your half-brother. I called him after you left yesterday, and he can't wait to see you either." When Russ showed Roger a picture of Sandy, he almost had a heart attack. Tears started running down his checks; he looked and looked at the picture, then kissed it. When he got his composure back, he said, "I'm sorry son, I just loved your mother so much, you can't believe how much I loved that women, can I have this picture if you have another one?"

"It's yours dad, I brought it just for you." Russ told him.

For the rest of the day Roger and Russ talked and talked. When Roger saw some other pictures of Sandy, he said "She is as pretty as I remembered she was. Later on that day, Roger took Russ over to the "Bar and Grill" and introduced his new son to everyone. After dinner that night, the two men took a long walk on the beach, that's when Russ got the phone call. He excused himself, and said "I have to take this call." After he hung up Russ looked at Roger and said, "I'm sorry, but I have to fly out as soon as possible. My son, your grandson, Robert is very sick and I have to go to him. I hope you understand, don't you? I promise I'll see you again now that I know where you live"

Roger drove his son to the Airport for the first flight to California. That would be the last time they would ever see one another. On the nightly news that night, there was a report that a small jet crashed in the mountains out west, with no survivors.

For the following two weeks Roger did nothing but drink, he drank in the morning, he drank in the afternoon and he drank at night, over at Rogg's Bar and Grill.

Gary and Sally were talking with him one night when she said, "This year has really been one hell of a year. First, Judy lost her son, than we lost Judy and now you lost your son. That damn Grim Reaper sure worked overtime this year."

After three long weeks Roger started to get over his depression. He was sitting at the Bar and Grill with all his friends, when a big black car turned into the parking lot and killed one of the chickens. Everyone stopped drinking to see who it was that just killed the chicken. A young man of about thirty got out of the car, looked at the dead chicken lying in the parking lot, then walked out back where everyone was sitting and enjoying an afternoon drink in the warm Florida sun. They all looked to see who just killed the chicken. A young man walked around to the back of the building and looked at everyone sitting on the patio, and then he said. "Who's Roger?"

After looking at the young man, Roger said, "I'm Roger."

Then the young man that just killed the chicken walked over to him and said, "Hello Grandpa, I'm Robert."

THE END

Printed in the United States
by Bookmasters

Printed in the United States
By Bookmasters